PRETTY BOY ROCK PRESENTS:
PHOENIX RISING
ISSUE #1

USA TODAY BESTSELLING AUTHORS
S.R. WATSON & RYAN STACKS

Phoenix Rising: Issue #1 (Pretty Boy Rock Series)

Copyright © 2020 S.R. Watson & Ryan Stacks

www.watsonandstacks.com

This book is a work of fiction. Names, characters, businesses, places, events, and incidents are either the product of the author's imagination or used fictitiously. Any resemblance to actual persons, living or dead, actual events or locales is entirely coincidental. The author acknowledges the trademark status and trademark owners of various products referenced in this work of fiction. The publication of these trademarks is not associated with or sponsored by the trademark owner.

All rights reserved. No part of this book may be reproduced, scanned, or distributed in any printed or electronic form without the express written permission of the author, except for the use of brief quotations in a book review. To obtain permission to excerpt portions of the text, please contact the authors at watsonandstacks@gmail.com

Cover Model: Shawn Dawson

Photographer: Allan Spiers

Editor: Editing4Indies

PROLOGUE

Phoenix

The dancing lights shining down on me are hot as fuck. My shirt clings to my chest from the sweat. My guys are going hard on the guitar and drums while I deliver these "Have Faith in Me" lyrics. We're on fire tonight! We rock Club Luxe every weekend, and it never gets old. "So, cling to what you know and never let go..." I make sure to make eye contact with the women standing front and center as I sing because one of them will be my conquest tonight. The eye contact personalizes the experience for them. *Or so they think.* We're on the second verse when I spot her. I don't know how I missed her come-hither eyes or that rack. Even with the lights in my eyes, I can see this sexy brunette with double D cleavage spilling over her midriff top and a skirt so short it barely covers her ass. I wink at her, and she blushes. The women to her right and her left blush too because they mistakenly think that wink was aimed for them. I'm sure they'd be down for a foursome, but this last set has me spent. I'm not in the mood to pleasure three women tonight. No, the sexy brunette is the lucky winner. I pull my shirt off over my head and watch as her eyes narrow. That telltale sign has sealed her fate. She will be on my cock before the bar closes.

OUR GIG FOR TONIGHT IS FINALLY FINISHED. I'M sitting in this makeshift backstage area designated for us by the bar. The room is a pretty decent size, so I can't complain. Not to mention, the owner, Steve, has tricked this room out with black and white leather sofas and other contemporary shit we don't need. All we need is a place to change and store our equipment, but he goes the extra mile to ensure we keep coming back. We fill the house every weekend with mostly horny women, thus bringing in the men too. It's a win-win. My thoughts are cut short by a timid knock on the door. Bandmates, Killian and Ren, have already left for an after-party with two chicks. Asher was the first to leave. He said something about grabbing a few things from the store before his stepsister arrived tomorrow. *It's after midnight, but okay.* The only person who it could be is my pussy for tonight. I had already given the green light to club security to let the brunette through if she came sniffing around backstage. I was beginning to think she wouldn't show—afraid of the possible rejection. Who am I kidding? I'm sure she is aware of her assets and how to work them. Women like that always get what they want. She is in for a surprise, though, because so do I. When she crosses the threshold of this room, I run the show.

MY SEXUAL APPETITE IS UNPARALLELED, AND SO ARE MY desires. Not every woman is privy to my tastes—I'm selective in that regard. I will have to see how this one behaves. If she submits, I'll tilt her world on its fucking axis. If she needs persuasion, I'll let her suck my cock before I show her the door. Those are the terms I live by.

Opening the door, I'm greeted with a wicked smile. Her intentions are written all over her face. "Hi," she says coyly. I'm not fooled by the innocent act, though.

"Come in. What is your name, sweetheart?" I step aside to let her in. The security guy gives me a thumbs-up before I close the door behind her.

"Shannon," she purrs. My eyes are drawn to her red lipstick with thoughts of those lips wrapped around my dick. "Nice dressing room," she adds.

"Thanks. So, what's on your mind, *Shannon?*" I ask, getting straight to the reason for her visit. I've never been one for pleasantries.

"Excuse me? What do you mean?"

"The reason you've come to my dressing room?" I can see she's trying to hold on to this coy act, but I'm not having it.

"Oh...well. I wanted to meet you. The other guys are great. I've been coming here for a while, but tonight was the first time I had a chance to be so close to the stage," she replies. *Such bullshit.* I hate liars and women who come back here, only to play innocent.

I~f~ ~you~ ~want~ ~to~ ~fuck~ ~me,~ ~own~ ~that~ ~shit.~ T~hat~ I ~can~ respect. I can smell how wet she is for me, yet she wants to hold on to this illusion of being a good girl. I'm about to shatter this little game she thinks she's playing.

"Nice meeting you, Shannon, but what I really want is to be sucked off. So, the way I see it, if you've gotten what you've come for, then there is the door. If you want to get me off, then get on your knees." I watch as hesitation crosses her face. She's probably not used to men being so blunt. Instead, she's used to them being wrapped around her finger. Her hesitation only lasts for a second before a smile crosses those lips. She drops to her knees, and her submission is enough to make me hard. I stroke my cock a few times, so she can watch it grow through my jeans. Her salivation is confirming everything I thought about her. *Good girl, my ass.* I take my dick out and rub it across her lips to tease her. She opens her mouth to take me in, but I pull back. *My show.*

"I say when, sweetheart," I tell her. I tease her a little more until a bead of pre-cum forms at the tip of my dick. She greedily licks it all up. "Open," I command. She does as I say with enthusiasm, so I let her take me to the back of her throat. *Holy shit.* Doesn't she have a gag reflex?

. . .

HER EXPERTISE AT SUCKING ME OFF HAS DEFINITELY given away that she is not new to this. Fuck, she is amazing. She bobs up and down on my length, and I can feel the tingling in my balls. I'm so close. I grab her by the hair to guide her for a few strokes before I try to pull her away. She refuses to be separated from my dick. I explode in her mouth, and she doesn't even flinch. She continues sucking and licking until she has every last drop. I let my shit throb for a few seconds while I watch the look of satisfaction on her face. I wasn't planning on fucking her, but she's earned it.

"Stand up and take that skirt off." She quickly stands and does as I say. This one is a quick learner. I reach over and pull her shirt underneath her tits. Damn, they're completely suckable, but I need to make this quick. The bar will be closing soon, and I need to be out of here before then.

"The panties, too?" she asks.

"Nope." I turn her around and bend her over the counter. Grabbing a condom from my pocket, I slide it on before pulling her panties to the side. Just as I thought. No priming needed because she's so wet. I slam into her, and she cries out in ecstasy. I fuck her hard and fast as her knees buckle. I knew this one would like it rough.

"Fuck, yes!" she screams. "Fuck me harder!" After I pound into her a few more times, she's coming all over my dick. The clench of her pussy is enough to pull me over the edge with her. After I'm done, I peel the condom off.

"Thanks, Shannon. It was really nice meeting you." I

wink. She smiles and begins grabbing her skirt and fixing her clothes. She knows her time has come to an end. I go into the bathroom adjacent from our dressing room to clean up a bit, and when I come back, she is gone. Asher has already taken the rest of my stuff back to the lake house with him, so I don't have anything to pack up. I grab my helmet from the corner and make my way outside to my bike. We play here again tomorrow night.

CHAPTER ONE

Harlow

This is ludicrous. Possibly the worst idea I've had yet. I've spent the past few years making sure I was invisible to the opposite sex, and now I'm going to live with four men for the summer. My stepbrother, Asher, has invited me to stay with him and his bandmates at their lake house before classes start this fall. We haven't seen each other in a few years and have only kept in touch by phone. I really miss Asher, but I question whether I can really go through with this. On the one hand, it is a chance of a lifetime. I will get to observe the journey of his band as they strive to get a record deal. If I'm going to be a music journalist, I need to know every aspect of the music business—not just the glamorous illusion, but also the road to fame. On the other hand, I'm awkward around men. To think about being around four of them absolutely petrifies me. Gah, why do I have to be such a chickenshit? I know Asher won't let these guys do anything to me. He's said so himself. They're all man whores, I'm sure. Their band name, Phoenix Rising, is probably synonymous with rising from some random's bed rather than from ashes. Either way, if I'm going to be successful in the business, I need to find a way to prohibit my past from crippling me. This just may be the therapy I need—a push out of my comfort zone.

I STAND HERE AT THE CURB OF THE ARRIVAL SECTION OF Birmingham Airport. Asher should be here at any moment to pick me up. My nerves are all over the place. I clutch my hot pink luggage tightly to redirect my focus. My luggage is the most colorful possession that I have. Black is my usual color of choice. From my baggy jeans to my black nail polish, everything I wear is black. The darkness matches my soul and my past. It keeps people away from me, especially men. I don't trust them. The only person to penetrate my fuck-off shield is Irelyn. She is my best friend and my complete opposite. We met at the community college I just transferred from, and from day one, she refused to be ignored. She didn't stop until she broke down my defenses. She thinks I'm just a cynic, but she only knows the lies that I told her to explain why I am the way that I am. The pink luggage was a gift from her, and a rebellious attempt to protest my black obsession. *Whatever.* A sleek, black Escalade pulls to a stop in front of me, interrupting my thoughts. Asher steps out of the SUV, and I swear he has hit a growth spurt. I don't remember him being so tall. He comes around the back of the SUV as he runs his hands through his blond hair. His cerulean blue eyes crinkle, and a frown creases his brows as he takes me in.

"WHAT THE HELL HAPPENED TO MY BABY SISTER?" HE jokes. There is an underlying seriousness in his tone. I've always had brunette hair, but now my waist-length tresses are blue-black from my home dye job. I'm told my hair makes my gray eyes look freakish. My hair is my veil to hide when I don't want to be seen. I'm not the girl he remembers from three years ago.

"What do you mean? It's still me," I chide. He begins putting my suitcases in the back as he shakes his head.

"Still you, but Gothified." He chuckles. "My princess has turned into Goth Barbie," he teases. Princess was the nickname he had for me before our parents separated, and Mom moved on to husband number three.

"Hush, you still love me. And Gothified is not even a word."

"Of course it is. I just need to get used to your new look." He closes the trunk and opens the passenger door for me. He is still the sweet guy I remember. Even though he is a little taller now, he's still lean like a swimmer. With his charm, I bet all the women swoon over him, but I don't want to think about him in that way. I want to keep my sweet image of my stepbrother pure. Hopefully, he's not a whore magnet like most guys in a band. Okay, to be fair, I don't know any guys in any band—all I know is what I see on TV.

"You're late, brother. This look is not new. This has been me since you left," I point out.

"Whatever, Goth girl, let's get you to your new home for the summer."

WITH THREE LEVELS AND A DECK THAT LEADS TO THE lake, this place is a dream. The main level is on the second floor, where I am now. The bedrooms are on the first and third floors. The furnishing and décor are contemporary and don't look like the home of rockers. Leave it to Mr. Nolan, Asher's dad, to spare no expense for these guys. That trait is what attracted my mom to him until she got greedy and went for a bigger fish. I think my favorite is the floor-to-ceiling windows in the living room, which let in all the natural light. The only thing missing is having Irelyn here with me. She is visiting family instead, and then she'll be transferring to the University of Alabama with me in the fall. I'm walking around the state-of-the-art kitchen and admiring the cherry wood cabinetry when the other bandmates arrive downstairs.

"The guys are here," Asher says excitedly. He hops up from the sofa and heads to go meet them and to clue them in that I'm here, I'm sure. The guys come upstairs in a boisterous manner, bantering about whom was going to put away the groceries they just bought. Asher introduces them to me, and I must say, my first impression is that they aren't as bad as I originally thought they'd be. So it seems. Killian Andrews is their lead guitarist, whereas Asher is the bass guitarist. Like my brother, Killian has shoulder-length hair, but his is brown like his chocolate eyes. Ren Lowry is their drummer. He has a black Mohawk and seems to be the only one who rivals my Gothness, as my brother would say. I'm digging his all-black attire. He gives me a slight chin lift as a greeting.

THE GUYS ARE ALL WELCOMING. THEY DON'T APPEAR TO be judging me for the way I look. I get that a lot, but it's kind of the point. I'm just about to ask who their singer is when he comes up the stairs. *Holy shit balls.* I wasn't ready. I hear Asher introducing him as Phoenix, but I'm speechless. Phoenix looks me up and down and smirks. I bet he gets this reaction from women all the time, but this is different. I don't fawn over men. They're not even on my radar. My heart quickens, and I work to swallow the lump in my throat. My nerves have kicked into overdrive. This feeling is foreign to me. This guy is so far from what you would expect as a singer of a rock band that it is unreal. He stands about six inches taller than my five-foot-four frame and is built like a fucking tank. The name Phoenix is so fitting for him. He is simply gorgeous. His shirt hugs his chest like a second skin, and I can see every etch of muscle. The tattoo sleeve on his left arm is an intricate work of art and draws your eyes even more to his fit physique. From his goatee to his perfectly styled short hair, he is perfection. His angled facial features are chiseled beauty. The fucker knows it, too. I can tell this one is going to be trouble. He arches an eyebrow in question, waiting for me to say something.

"Hi. Nice to meet you," I manage to say without getting tongue-tied. Geesh, I feel like an idiot. He is just a good-looking guy. *Get it together.* "Where is my room?" I ask, turning toward Asher. I'm going to have to stay far away from this Phoenix guy. The others seem nice enough, but my gut is telling me that he is trouble with a capital T.

"The guys and I discussed it. You can take the master bedroom on the third floor," Asher says. A look passes between him and Phoenix before he grabs my luggage to take them upstairs. Phoenix follows us up the stairs.

"They discussed it," he comments. "That was my room. I got booted to the room next door, so don't think you're going to get that bathroom all to yourself," he informs. I don't want to come in taking over their space, so I just nod and look away as we pass the only other bedroom on this floor.

. . .

"There are two more bathrooms in the house, Phoenix," Asher chastises.

"Yeah, but I want to use that one. That is the only master bathroom and the only one with a rain shower. Don't worry; I won't bother your *princess*. She is not my speed anyway." Phoenix smirks. Asher's face hardens, and I know he is getting ready to put his foot down. The last thing I want is to cause problems on my first day here. I can't believe he told them he calls me princess, but like Phoenix just confirmed, I'm not his type anyway. I grab Asher's arm to shush him.

"It's fine. Really. I'm sure he and I can set up some sort of schedule. We're the only two rooms up here, so it's no problem," I assure.

"Whatever. You don't have to agree to that. You're the only female in the house and should have your privacy—"

"Don't make this awkward," I plead, cutting off his rant. I look over at Phoenix, and his smugness is revolting. He didn't win. I just don't want any special privileges or to upset the balance of the house.

. . .

"Fine. One complaint and he's out," Asher promises.

"I've yet to have a woman complain about anything that concerns me." Phoenix winks. He leaves the room chuckling.

"Fuck," Asher groans as he leaves the room with him.

I take a look around the room now that I'm alone. This bedroom is huge. It has a sitting area as well as doors that lead to a balcony overlooking the lake. More floor-to-ceiling windows compliment the space. The four-poster bed looks inviting until I imagine all the kinky sex that has taken place in it. I shudder at the thought as I walk into the en suite bathroom. Somehow, I knew it would be a dream. I can see why Phoenix didn't want to give it up. The rustic travertine tiled shower, encased in glass, could fit like ten people. I see the rain shower that he spoke about next to a regular showerhead. It even has a bench in there. *Interesting.* The Jacuzzi tub sitting off to the side of the shower is the icing on the cake. I know where I'll be spending a lot of my time. I love to soak and read. Well, more like an escape into a different realm of reality and pretend I'm the heroine who gets the happily ever after—not the dysfunctional life I have.

First, I guess I'll unpack. The walk-in closet within the master bath is massive. I flip the light on and am shocked to already see men's clothing hung up and sneakers lining the wall. So, it appears he hasn't cleared the space yet, or does he want to share the closet, too? It's definitely big enough. It's almost big enough to be a sixth bedroom. *Whatever.* I'll just grab my favorite romance novel and read for now. I push the suitcases against the opposite wall as his shoes and grab my book out of my bag. I walk back into the bedroom and curl up into the oversize chair next to the window. I'm not getting in that bed until I change the sheets—just in case.

CHAPTER TWO

Phoenix

The guys are discussing what songs we're going to cover tonight from the band, I Prevail. Honestly, I'm tired of singing other people's shit, but our music is not ready yet. We only have one original song that we perform, titled "Something to Believe In." I write all of our music, and that song has special meaning since it's the first one I started working on. It has significance to my past, but the guys just think it is a badass song. We don't play it every set, but when we do, we play it to close the night, and it brings down the fucking house every time. The topic changes to what after-hours club they plan on hitting up tonight after our show, and I smile as I think about Asher's *"princess"* upstairs.

. . .

I'VE OVERHEARD HIM CALL HER THAT NICKNAME. IT WAS odd as shit, to say the least, to hear the word come out of a grown man's mouth. Imagine my surprise when this princess arrives dressed from head to toe in black, looking as dark as my soul. I see the Goth image, but something is amiss. I just can't put my finger on it yet. I saw the instant attraction she had for me, yet she chose to pretend otherwise. The shift of her eyes toward the ground when I speak to her gives her away. I'd kill to know what thoughts ran through her mind. What she must think of me? I'm very aware of how most women see me. They want any opportunity to fuck me, and some even want to "tame the bad boy." *Fucking hysterical.* Not her, though. I can tell little Miss Harlow is planning on staying the hell away from me. Too bad it's a challenge I'm willing to accept even though she's not really my type.

I GOT A PEEK AT WHAT SHE REALLY DESIRES, AND I PLAN on opening her up. I bet she has a hot body under all those baggy clothes. Those piercing gray eyes of hers got my attention. It's going to be fun exploring the rest of her. Asher has warned us all off her, so she will have to come to me, but she will. She will submit. In the end, they all do. Yup, my summer just got a little more interesting.

I WATCH AS SHE COMES DOWNSTAIRS. APPARENTLY, SHE is coming to tonight's gig. This should be fun. I hope she'll be in the front row. She is in for a treat. I have a special performance just for her. This will be the real test. She looks around nervously, and I almost feel sorry for her. *Almost.*

"Ready for tonight, princess?" I ask cheekily as we load the Escalade with our equipment.

"Don't call me that," Harlow whisper hisses. Hmm, so she has some bite. I don't mind. Even better.

"Why not? Asher calls you that. You don't like it?"

"It's condescending when you say it," she points out.

"It isn't meant to be." I smirk. "It's just so fitting," I continue while gesturing toward her all-black appearance. She huffs and walks around to the other side of the SUV.

So the goal is not to get under her skin. No, I want to get under something else completely. The more she resists me, the harder my dick gets. This feeling is foreign to me. Women usually make this shit too easy. I won't lie and say it isn't great to have my pick of pussy, but a challenge may be just what I need for a change of pace. I have to be careful not to get too involved, though. The last thing I need is to have her fall in love with me. Asher really would kick my ass if I break his sister's heart. No. Get in and get out. That's the challenge. My dick accepts.

CHAPTER THREE

Harlow

I sip on my mojito, which I have been nursing for the past thirty minutes as I sit here at the bar. Some Layla chick has been refilling my drink every time it gets low. I'm guessing the only reason I haven't been carded is because she knows I'm with the band. Asher introduced me at the start of the night. Well, I'll be twenty-one in a year anyway, so who cares? Two beers and two mojitos later, the guys are finally preparing to take the small stage in the back of the room. The mob of women rushing in that direction tips me off that it's showtime. I slam back the remaining contents in my glass and head toward the side of the stage where I can see but be away from the drunken women ready to throw their panties. Their drunken squeals are somewhat comical. The lights dim as the strobe lights begin to dance. Smoke seeps from the edge of the stage, and I have to say I'm impressed with the effects. The drummer, Ren, starts with a sexy rhythmic tempo followed by a familiar melody strummed by Asher. By the time Killian's chords are added to the mix, I'm sure that I know this song, but I can't put my finger on it. That is, until Phoenix's lips sing the first lyric. *Holy. Fucking. Shit.* The arrangement is different, but it is Jeremih's "Fuck You All the Time" song.

PHOENIX WALKS TO THE END OF THE STAGE AND SCANS the crowd until he finds me. His jeans hug his ass in the most sinful way while his plain white T-shirt shows off every etched muscle perfectly. The stage lights shine down on him, and he is standing there looking quite sexy. The women compete for a second of his attention—just for a quick glance. They're shaking their breasts and hollering obscene things, but he doesn't seem the least bit fazed. His eyes finally lock with mine as he sings the seductive lyrics, and I'm paralyzed at the moment. I want to look away, but I simply can't. The rock undertones give this song an edge, and it is equal parts sensual. One of Phoenix's eyebrows arches in question as I flush crimson from the visual. My brain is telling me he is a narcissistic douche, but the ache he is causing between my legs with each lyric that falls from those gorgeous lips is saying otherwise. My kitty will lose this battle, though. I won't be like the women he is used to and just part my legs for him. I'm sure the alcohol coursing through my blood right now is a contributing factor to this moment of lust.

His hands caress his abs. He makes sure that his shirt raises just enough to give us a peek at his V-cut muscles, which disappear into his jeans, now riding low on his hips.

EVEN FROM THIS DISTANCE, MY EYES HONE IN ON A VEIN that lies along that muscle. I don't know why I find it uber sexy. As a matter of fact, I don't know why I'm turned on at all. I've been holding on to my celibacy for the past two years. It's my superpower. I use it, in addition to my fuck-off appearance, to repel men and their one-track mind.

"*I could fuck you all the time,*" Phoenix reaches the chorus, and the screams from the women reach another octave.

"You can fuck me, Phoenix," a thirsty redhead yells over the crowd. I watch in disbelief as she flashes her perfectly round, sizable breasts—purchased, I'm sure. He winks at her, and a devious smile forms on his lips. He grabs his crotch as an acknowledgment and continues the suggestive lyrics. Witnessing all of this is like cold water being doused on my libido. *Ugh, what a manwhore.* I make my way back to the bar to get another drink. I'm happy to plant my butt in this chair until the guys are done. I don't need a front row seat to the sex-crazed freak show. I can follow their journey without being in the midst of it all. I can observe from a distance. It is more than apparent that these guys are beyond talented. It is equally apparent all of the pussy they must have thrown at them.

. . .

The band plays a number of songs, but I have lost count. I watched as they each flirt with the crowd in a game of seduction, but Phoenix was definitely the worst by far. He has a sex appeal that is incomparable, and he knows it. Asher seems to be the tamest of them all, but that may be just for my benefit. The guys wrap up the last of their set and head toward the back, which I'm guessing doubles as a dressing room. I take my time finishing my mojito before I get up to go join them. I have already been introduced to the bar's security, so they know that I'm Asher's stepsister as well.

The security guy on for tonight is named Albert. He gives me a puzzled look as if he is wondering if he should just let me through, but then he moves aside and lets me pass. The hallway is narrow, and there are only a few rooms back here. I can hear the music behind one of the doors, so I'm guessing that is where the guys are. I knock a few times, but there is no answer. I hear laughter from one of the guys, so I know they're in there. The music blaring is keeping them from hearing me. I turn the knob, the door is unlocked, so I push the door open. It takes them a moment to see that I just walked in. The sight before me is shocking, to put it lightly.

My eyes zero in on Phoenix first. He has a blonde on her knees, sucking him off. He gives me a small smirk while the hand he has tangled in her hair pushes her mouth farther down on his cock to take him deeper. The girl doesn't seem fazed by the intrusion. Ren and Killian both have their own groupie whores on their laps wearing clothes so skimpy they're laughable. Judging by their position, they're well on their way to their own sex act, and I'm interrupting. The guys look at me and then at each other before Killian finally speaks up.

"Asher is out back with a few friends, putting our gear in the truck if you want to join him," he suggests. I'm not stupid. It is his nice way of saying we're trying to get our fuck on, and you're in the way. The two women's glacial stares clue me in that they ready for me to hurry the hell up because I'm taking the attention away from them.

"Oh, okay," I say, playing along. I refuse to look over at Phoenix again. The groans coming from him are sickening. This is definitely not my scene. I wouldn't be surprised if they plan on swapping. All of this while Asher puts all of their shit away. I turn to get the hell out of this room before I lose it. Asher needs to put his foot down.

CHAPTER FOUR

Harlow

I find Asher out back, putting the last of their equipment in the Escalade as Killian said.

He's deep in conversation with a guy he introduces as Nick. Nick is a lanky-looking kid with hair that he keeps wiping from his eyes. His need for a haircut is evident. Apparently, he is the son of the owner, Steve. He helps the guys set up and take down when they come to play.

"Asher, why do you let them make you do all the work?" I question when Nick disappears back into the bar.

"They don't make me do anything. I make myself scarce. I have someone I'm seeing in San Diego, so I'm trying to stay away from the extracurricular that goes on after the shows," he admits. "I could wait until they finish with the groupies to pack up, but this helps to pass the time, and I have Nick to help, so I just get it over with." I get what he's saying, and it makes sense, but it still seems like they get to play while he works.

"Well, if I'm going to be going to these gigs with you guys, I can help you pack up. Those women are deplorable and lack even the slightest hint of morals," I offer.

"Why? What did you see?" Asher pauses and looks at me intently. I have stuck my foot in my mouth. I don't want to be labeled as the tattletale.

"I saw how those women behaved while you guys were playing. That one woman flashed her tits, ugh." Asher breathes a sigh of relief and chuckles.

Somehow, his reaction makes me believe what I witnessed, just now, is only the tip of the iceberg of shenanigans they get into.

"You don't have to, but I won't turn down the company," he says as he opens the truck door for me.

"Good. Now tell me about this woman you're seeing." Asher's whole face lights up. It must be pretty serious.

. . .

"Her name is Lily, and she is an amazing woman," he begins. He tells me how they met after another one of his gigs, and she was sitting in a hotel lobby, waiting for her whorish friends to finish hooking up with the other band members. Asher waited with her, so she wouldn't have to be a part of that scene, and they hit it off. That was three months ago, and they've kept in contact ever since. She is supposed to fly out for a visit in a couple of weeks, so I'll get a chance to meet her.

"I'm glad you're not like the others," I confess to Asher.

"Don't give me too much credit. Before Lily, I'd participated in my share of sexcapades. It just gets old, you know?" He shakes his head as he recalls the memories. "Those guys are still young and single. As long as the women are willing and don't have any expectations of more than one night of sex, I don't have any problems with it. The guys aren't into drugs—we have a strict policy against that. Everything else is small potatoes."

Asher proceeds to tell me a little about each of the band members and how they all met. I was shocked to learn he met Phoenix through Killian. Phoenix and Killian used to work together as bartenders. Asher and

Killian had been working on music and the plan to start a band for a couple of years before Killian discovered that Phoenix could sing late one night at the bar. He told him about their band idea and asked if he would be interested in joining as their lead singer. Phoenix was hesitant at first but was quickly swayed once he heard the guys play a few cover songs. Phoenix knew a guy from school who could play bass guitar, and from there, the band was formed. Unlike I previously thought, the band's name was derived from their collective plans to rise from the ashes—from the cards they were dealt.

We talk about their dreams and the future of the band. Phoenix is their frontman and writes all their songs. They're still a work in progress, so only one song has been shared during their gigs. Right now, they are just playing cover songs and looking for management to take them to that next level. Currently, it is all on Phoenix's shoulders. He can play guitar too—multitalented and kinky, it seems. He is an enigma to me. I've seen firsthand the attention women give and how he reciprocates, but something still makes him alluring to me. My skin prickles at the thought of his name. I would never act on it, but my traitorous body definitely defies my insistence on not being attracted to him.

. . .

I change the subject, and we talk about my mother and marriage number three. I can't stand him. Thomas is a real fucking tool. I don't want to get into my hatred for him. I steer the conversation back to the good memories, when his dad was still married to my mom and having him with me—a time before the Goth as he calls it. Time passes quickly, and it is not long before we're being interrupted by the guys, who have now come out of the bar to head home. They've ditched their one-night stands. Phoenix slides in the back behind Asher, who is in the driver's seat. I'm in the passenger seat, but I can feel Phoenix's stare.

"I'm starving," Ren says, sliding in next to Phoenix. "What are we getting to eat?" Asher looks over at me.

"Oh, it doesn't matter. Whatever everyone else wants is fine." My buzz has worn off, and I admit I am kind of hungry.

"Pizza it is then," he says, and everyone mumbles in agreement. The guys try to talk in code about the orgy they just had, and once again, I feel like an intruder. Surprisingly, Phoenix is quiet and doesn't participate in the replay of it all. It's going to take some time to get used to listening to the guy talk, but it's a beneficial inside track for my journalism. I lay my head against the seat and pretend not to hear about what redhead number one could do with her tongue. I close my eyes and drown out their sounds with my own thoughts that hold me captive. After all this time, the more unpleasant ones still manage to make a daily appearance. Nobody knows about these demons but me, and that is where they will stay. They can't hurt me by memories alone.

I'M READY TO CALL IT A NIGHT. I TOOK A BRIEF WALK down to the lake when we got back while the guys headed to the first floor for a meeting. The combination of listening to music and going for a walk always works to clear my head. Now I just want a soak in the tub and hit the bed. I walk into the bathroom, engulfed in the music still playing from my earbuds. My step falters when I realize I'm not alone. Phoenix is in the shower with his back to me. Holy shit, what a fucking sight! My feet are frozen in place as I watch rivulets of water stream down his back. I watch as the corded muscles in his thighs bunch with the slightest of movement. His ass is perfection—who am I kidding? His entire body is perfection. His egotistical ways are his only flaw. I know I'm intruding again, and I should leave, but I can't stop admiring this specimen of a man. He must feel my presence because he turns slightly until his eyes lock with mine. He leans forward against the tile, but he doesn't utter a single word. *Fuck, I can't move.* It's like watching a train wreck. Phoenix turns to face me, and I will my eyes not to look down. *Epic Fail...Motherfucker.* His cock is so hard and juts upward toward his navel. The immediate ache between my legs lets me know that I'm not immune to him—no matter how hard I try to be. His thick length has me salivating. I'm not sure who this woman is that he has awakened in me.

"See something you want, Harlow?" he finally says. His knowing tone is enough to break me from his invisible hold. I run out of there quickly, knowing my hand has been shown.

CHAPTER FIVE

Phoenix

I'm sitting here in the living room, writing the lyrics for our newest song, "Come Undone." The guys have all gone out to hang with friends, but it's been a minute since I've had any inspiration for this song. I've been stuck in one particular spot, and now that the verses are flowing, I have to get them down. I'm on a roll until last night's events creep into my thoughts. I picture Harlow standing there while I shower. The heat smoldering in her eyes was very telling. She wants me and doesn't even know it. Either that or she's just in denial. While she watched me perform at the bar, her body language was one of intrigue mixed with jealousy—jealous of the attention that I gave the women. The flush of her face when she saw another woman sucking my cock was just as revealing. I watched as her eyes wandered around the room at the other bandmates, and her reaction to their conquests was not the same. All of these instances told me what I already figured. I can't help but smile because I know it is only a matter of time before I have my way. My allure is strong. Like all the others, she will come to me once she gives in to what her body craves—me. Deep down, all women want to conquer the bad boy. I can appreciate the challenge as I enjoy watching her at war with her wants and desires. I won't make it easy for her. She will submit willingly.

I HEAR HER COMING DOWN THE STEPS, SO I CONTINUE writing the hook I was just working on. A quick glimpse is all I need to see she is wearing all black again. A baggy shirt and baggy pants hide her frame, but her hair is pulled back in a ponytail today.

"Something smells good," she mentions. So I guess we're going to pretend last night didn't happen.

"Yeah. I have some tilapia baking in the oven. Today is meal prep Sunday."

"What is meal prep Sunday?" she asks, walking toward the kitchen. I lay my notebook down, take my headphones off, and join her. She looks at me inquisitively, and I'm blown away by how beautiful her eyes are. They're piercing gray and looking right at me now.

"Sunday is the day I prep my meals for the entire week. I need to eat every three hours to support my metabolism and muscle growth," I explain.

"You have enough muscles." She gestures by pointing

at my arms. Those beautiful grays roam my body before she realizes she's staring and looks away. " I've never seen a singer in a rock band look like you before," she admits.

"Well, good. Mission accomplished. I don't want to look like your typical rocker."

"Anyway, I'm sure you can eat whatever you want," she concludes. She looks over the pan of chicken breast and greens I have already set aside. "You had pizza last night."

"It's about balance. I don't aim to be lean year-round. I have days that I allow myself to indulge, but your training won't erase a bad diet. I have to make conscious decisions of what I'm putting into my body and work out."

I TAKE THE TILAPIA OUT OF THE OVEN, AND SHE ASKS how she can help. I grab a few of the Tupperware containers and pass them to her. I tell her how many ounces of the prepped food go into each of the containers. I don't meal prep my breakfast, but I do have a shit ton of eggs that I put into a zip lock bag. She inspects the bag but doesn't say a word. We take turns using the scale and fall into a rhythm of portioning and sealing my food. I've never shared this task with a woman before—or anyone really. Nobody has really taken an interest, let alone ask to help. The guys don't eat what I eat, so it doesn't make a difference to them.

"So what were you working on when I came downstairs?" Harlow inquires.

"Just working on some of our music. Some lyrics for a song came to me, and I needed to get them down."

"What is the name of the song?" Her face lights up with curiosity.

"'Come Undone.'"

"I love music and writing. It is the reason I want to combine the two and be a music journalist. Can I hear some of it?" While I find it amusing that I'm actually talking about something other than sex with a female, my music process is private. I don't even share with the guys until it's done. They provide a soundtrack for me, and I provide the lyrics to said track.

IN SOME INSTANCES, I WRITE LYRICS AND THEN HELP the guys lay tracks to what I've written.

"Hmm, I don't share until it's complete. I will tell you that I'm sampling a little from the original "Come Undone" by Duran Duran. It's a group from the eighties, so you may not be familiar with them."

"Of course I am. Music lover, remember?" She gives me this megawatt smile, and I can help but laugh. With her fist to her mouth like a microphone, she sing a line from the song. I can't do anything but stare. She drops her hand, embarrassed.

"You have a nice voice," I compliment. "Don't be embarrassed." She lets her guard down for a moment, and I get a peek at the woman behind all this black. She hasn't been here with us long, but I can tell she puts up a front that she hides behind. I suddenly have an urge to know more about her. What is she hiding? Who hurt her? I bet that's what it is—an old boyfriend maybe. She is not like all the other women I meet, and it is refreshing. It makes me want her even more, but not enough to change my own rules. She will have to come to me. Until then, nothing will happen between us.

"Thank you," she says shyly.

WE GET ALL OF MY FOOD PREPPED AND PACKED AWAY, so I ask for her help to make dinner. I admit that I'm enjoying her company. Usually, any woman in my presence equates to fucking and me leaving. None of the guys have women over because this is our sanctuary. No drama from pop-up visits or women who want more. Besides, if you go to their place, you can just leave. You don't have to worry about how you're going to kick them out. Regardless, anyone that gets the dick knows the score. A nut or two is the most that I can offer, and then I'm out. It may make me a bastard, but at least I'm an honest one. I don't do relationships. I'm in control at all times, and I decide who is worth pleasuring. I can tell with Harlow things are different. I'm up for a challenge. I genuinely enjoy her company, so I don't mind waiting until she acts upon what she really wants.

"Sure. What are we cooking?" she asks. "You're not going to eat any of this food you just prepared?"

"Oh, I am. This is for the guys. I normally cook for

everybody on Sundays since I'm already in the kitchen," I explain. "I was thinking of chicken cacciatore."

"That sounds out of my recipe repertoire." She giggles and then looks away. I'm going to enjoy bringing her out of her shell—bringing down these walls she has put up. I don't comment on my observation of her bouts of shyness; I simply take note.

"No. I promise it's not that hard. I got the recipe off the Food Network," I assure. "Can you cook?"

"Somewhat. Nothing that fancy."

"Well, get ready to learn, woman," I say as I wink at her. Her face flushes crimson. Also noted. I begin to pull more chicken out of the fridge with all the other ingredients we need. "The flour is key and for the dredging," I explain.

"What the heck is dredging?" She sighs.

"It's the same as breading. It's the mixture we will make to coat the chicken to make it extra flavorful, and oh so delicious."

"Yeah, but you can't have any," Harlow points out.

"Don't remind me. I already had pizza last night." I fake a facepalm, and it earns me another giggle from her. I'm starting to like the sound of it. "Well, I just have to live vicariously through your taste buds."

"I'll be sure to tell you how wonderful it tastes," she teases. I continue to go over the ingredient list with her

PHOENIX RISING: ISSUE #1

while we prep. It only takes us about twenty minutes. I sauté the onion, bell pepper, and garlic before instructing her to add the dry white wine. Once we add the oregano, capers, chicken broth, and tomatoes, we leave it all to simmer. "This is fun," she admits. I have to agree.

"Shush, don't tell anyone. That's my other secret talent," I joke.

"What is your other secret talent?" she questions.

THE DEVIOUS SMILE THAT SPREADS ACROSS MY LIPS GIVES away where my mind has deviated. I show her my tongue as I stretch it to touch my chin. "Good God. Never mind," she says, rolling her eyes.

"What?" I ask innocently.

"You know what. This has been a good time. Don't taint it with your manwhore insinuations. I don't need to know how well you eat pussy," she huffs. Hearing the word "pussy" come out of that pretty little mouth of hers cracks me up for some reason. The vile word is at odds with the underlying innocence she keeps hidden. She is not yet comfortable with her sexuality, and I can tell. It's a turn-on because she when does submit to me and her desires, it will be an experience that she hasn't shared with many. While I don't think she is a virgin, I do believe her body count is extremely low. Most men wouldn't take the time to get past all the defenses. I, on the other hand, have all the time in the world. I have no shortage of pussy thrown at me daily. The opportunity to conquer hers can play out simultaneously in a game of wills.

"Ah, but you're the one who took it there. I never said anything about eating pussy, or how good I am at it—glad you think so, by the way. I was simply showing you my tongue. How many people can touch their chin with their tongue? That's the talent I was speaking of."

SHE KNOWS I'M FULL OF SHIT, BUT SHE CAN'T PROVE IT. She smirks, and I laugh. I have to admit, I'm quite good at cunnilingus, but so few have the opportunity to find out. I refuse to put my mouth on the easy pussy thrown at me. I'm selective in that regard. That pleasure is reserved for the woman I'm in a relationship with, and since that has been a while, so has the exercise of my oral talents. *Hypocritical...maybe.*

"Whatever. That's not a talent."

She's obviously flustered at the thought of me pleasuring another woman, so I change the subject. "So tell me about growing up with Asher." He has already told this story. I know his dad was her mom's second marriage, and they were together for three years. She was in the sixth grade at the time, and he was in the ninth. Their parents split up his senior year. He went off to college for a bit, but they kept in touch. Even though I know most of the story, I want to put her back in her comfort zone.

It works. She tells me all about how even though he

was the protective older brother and annoyed her at times, he was the best brother a girl could have. *God, if he only knew the thoughts that ran through my mind about his baby sister—well, stepsister, but still.* That is a fine line I will gladly walk, and another reason anything happening between us will definitely have to be her idea—or so she will think.

"What about you? I hear that you met Asher through Killian."

"Yeah. Killian and I worked at this shitty bar in Birmingham. Our conversations eventually led to our love for music. We discovered that he played the guitar and that I sing as well as write music. He told me a friend of his was looking to form a band." She listens intently as I tell her all about our formation. The food finishes cooking, so I fix her a plate. I can feel her looking at me as she takes a seat at the counter.

"Come on. I'm bringing your plate into the living room. I'm going to watch one of my recordings of *American Horror Story*."

"I don't watch scary movies," she insists as she hesitantly walks behind me.

I set her plate on the coffee table as I take a seat on the sofa. I pat the space next to me and motion for her to come sit next to me. "Come on, pussy. It's not that bad. It's not scary the way you think." She sits next to me, and I hand her the plate of food.

"I'm not a pussy," she exclaims. She takes the food from me and takes the first bite. I'm scrolling through the recordings when a moan escapes her lips. My dick jumps to attention immediately. *Holy fuck.* I can't help but imagine myself fucking her and having that sweet sound be the result of my cock buried so deep inside her.

"Sorry," she mumbles when she realizes her mistake. "This is really good."

"Orgasmic, I guess," I tease. She rolls her eyes. "Hey, you're the one moaning. I'll take that as a compliment."

"It's amazing, and I helped."

"Yes, you did." I wink. She sighs, and I manage not to laugh. She is so cute, even with the Goth bullshit she's trying to pull off. I have no problem with the look or people who are actually into the lifestyle. I can just tell that her impersonation is just that—an act. I've had friends who were truly Goth and were cool as shit. She is an imposter, but I won't call her out on it. I finally find the "Curtain Call" episode. I fill her in briefly on the premise of the show. She comments on them calling themselves freaks, but other than that, she watches along with me and finishes her food.

She doesn't make the whole hour without dozing off. I know I should either wake her up to go lie down upstairs or let her have the sofa, but I can't help myself. I put a pillow on my lap and ease her head down until she lays on me. I lean back and flip to a recording of *Key and Peele*.

This act is beyond what I'm capable of, but Harlow has been different from the beginning. I can't put my finger on it yet. I watch as her breathing evens out. She's so vulnerable at this moment with no pretenses. The door rattles on the first floor, and I know the guys are back. Ren's hearty laugh confirms this. *Shit.*

CHAPTER SIX

Harlow

A door slamming in the distance startles me awake. I look up into the eyes of Phoenix. Crap, I was lying on his lap. How in the hell did that happen? I let myself get too comfortable with him. I jump up and grab my plate. "Sorry," I say.

"It's no big deal, Harlow. You were tired," Phoenix offers. He gets up and stretches, and I take my plate to the kitchen. The sun sits low in the sky now. Phoenix and I had an enjoyable day together. Who would have guessed? He had a few slip-ups, but for the most part, I got a chance to see another side to him besides the manwhore who encourages the women to be thirsty. Yes. I kind of like the Phoenix I got to spend time with today. Falling asleep in his lap was my mistake, and I'll just have to be more careful. I hope he didn't take that as me flirting. Although we made a few strides toward a possible friendship, I'm not fooled to think he is anything but a slut who enjoys all the pussy he wants. I'm not one of those females who idiotically thinks they have the power to change a man. A man only has the power to change if he wants to, and I don't see that for Phoenix. He is gorgeous, and he knows it. He has the world at his feet, and when these guys make it big, because they will, the number of women who throw themselves at him will increase exponentially.

Asher, Ren, and Killian come into the kitchen and excitedly grab a plate.

"Chicken cacciatore. Hell, yes!" Asher fist bumps with Ren. "Hey, sis. Did you get to taste this masterpiece? It's our favorite."

"Yes. It's quite good." I giggle. "And I helped."

"Well, it should be twice as good," Asher jokes. Ren and Killian mumble in agreement with their mouths full. I can see the camaraderie among them. I rinse my plate and put it into the dishwasher before heading upstairs. I play around on my laptop for a bit, mostly looking to see what my old friends are up to on Facebook. The two-hour time difference from Los Angles is catching up with me. It isn't long before I feel my eyes growing heavy. Maybe I'll just take a small nap and then get up and plan what classes I'll be registering for in a couple of weeks.

∽

THE SUN SHINING BRIGHTLY THROUGH MY CURTAINS IS A clue that I missed the mark on a small nap. I sit up and feel around for my phone. It only has nine percent since I didn't charge it last night. Damn, it's almost eight. That was some nap. After plugging in my phone, I poke my head out the door but find the house completely silent. I wonder where the guys went this morning? I pull out a pair of Easy Rider sweatpants to wear with my combat boots and an extra-large plain black tee.

I BRING IT ALL TO THE BATHROOM ALONG WITH SOME undergarments and set it down on the counter. I wash off yesterday's makeup while the water in the shower gets hot. I step in, and the rain shower is heaven. I wash my hair and spend at least twenty minutes indulging in the warmth before finally showering and getting out. I'm toweling myself dry when Phoenix walks in unexpectedly. I have just enough time to back myself against the glass shower and cover my front with the small ass towel I had in my hand.

"What the fuccc—?" he asks, obviously startled by my presence. It's deja vu in reverse.

"Get out, Phoenix!" I shout. He stands there, blinking as he looks me up and down.

"I can't believe this is what was under all that heavy makeup and baggy clothes. Then again, I knew it."

"I'm not having this conversation with you right now. Please get out," I beg. I'm near tears as he sees me in my most vulnerable state. It's not my near nakedness, but the absence of my armor. The armor that keeps men from being attracted to me. I don't want anybody to see me.

"Okay. Fine. We need to set up a bathroom schedule, though." He backs out with his eyes on me the entire time. Once he is out, I run to the door and turn the lock on the door. This was my fault. I can't believe I didn't lock the fucking door. I'm living with four men.

I THROW MY CLOTHES ON IN A FLASH. IT WOULD BE MY luck that the one person I didn't want to see me without my armor is the one who did. The last thing I need is for him to coming sniffing my way. It's not that I think I'm some catch, by any means, but guys always want the very thing they can't have—the thrill of the chase. The women who clamor over him are way sexier than I could ever hope to be in my wildest dreams. Let him stick with those women in his league. I'm determined not to make this weird. After all, it was just like me walking in on him yesterday and gawking like a horny teenager. One good turn deserves another. I know he isn't going to let this go, though. All I can do is put my face and armor back on, and act like I don't give a rat's ass about what he saw—which wasn't much, body-wise.

When I walk out into the hall, the house is once again quiet. They're obviously here somewhere, so I head downstairs to investigate. Just as I reach the bottom step to the first floor, the door across from me swings open.

Ren walks past me to head upstairs. Asher didn't get a chance to show me this room during the brief tour of the house he gave me because I was too infatuated with the second floor and the lake out back. I can clearly see now that they have the room set up as their makeshift studio.

MY EARS PERK UP AT PHOENIX'S RASP AS HE SINGS INTO the mic he's holding. "*You call the shots, babe. I just wanna be yours.*" He sings the lyrics to Arctic Monkey's, "I Wanna Be Yours," and I swear he's singing them to me. His stare pierces through me. Without all the noise of the women competing for his attention, I can focus strictly on his voice. The timbre of his voice is enthralling—so raw and captivating. He could sing the fucking *Yellow Pages* and get my attention. He closes his eyes as he gets lost in the lyrics, and I take this moment to stare. His body sways to the sexiness of the music. His denim jeans are snug against his muscular legs, and his black tank shows the work he puts in the gym. His chiseled chest begs to be caressed. God, this man makes me crazy. My thoughts are all over the damn place. I want to hold on to my comfort zone, yet he inspires all kinds of lustful thoughts. Not that I would act on any of them or even admit it to him, but damn he is insanely fucking sexy. I need to get my shit together. Nothing changes. Status quo. I don't have time for men. I have goals, and men are not part of the plan. I will just ogle privately, but that is as far as I'm willing to take it. Simply put—nice eye candy.

. . .

I don't realize I'm just standing in the doorway like a goof until Asher walks over to me.

"What do you need, Harlow?" he whispers, never missing a chord.

"Oh. I just came to see where everyone was," I whisper back.

"Our practice sessions are closed. The guys need to be able to concentrate." His eyebrows scrunch in concern. "Sorry."

"No worries. I see you guys are busy. I'm going back upstairs." Ren walks back in with a jug of water.

"We'll be wrapping up in about an hour...okay?"

"Sure," I tell Asher. He closes the door, and the sound is very faint now. You definitely wouldn't be able to hear it upstairs. The riddle is solved. They're in a soundproof room. I go back upstairs and try to decide what to do with myself. I'm bored. Then I get the brilliant idea to cook the guys breakfast. I don't know if they ate already, but the kitchen doesn't smell like it unless they ate out. Oh well, hopefully not. I pull out a carton of eggs, veggies, and even luck out and find some ham. I know Phoenix can't have a regular omelet, so I separate some egg whites for him. I spray coconut oil into a skillet and make omelets for the guys with all the fixings. Then I make an egg white omelet for Phoenix with just veggies. I put on a pot of coffee and make scrambled eggs for myself. I'm mid-bite when the guys come up the stairs.

. . .

"What smells so good?" Ren asks.

"I made you guys all omelets. Phoenix, I made you an egg white omelet with veggies. I used coconut oil to coat the pan to keep it healthy for you."

"Look at Phoenix getting special treatment already," Ren jokes.

"Thank you, Harlow." Phoenix smiles. "Are you trying to outshine me with the fellas?"

"Hush. No," I say, punching him in the arm softly. Holy crap. He is solid.

Asher ignores the flirtatious undertone Ren is trying to insinuate. "Thank you for breakfast, princess. Especially since I kicked you out of our practice," he says apologetically.

"Yeah, princess," the guys echo in unison. Ugh. Asher needs to stop calling me princess in front of these guys. They can be so childish.

"Not a problem at all," I reply. I grab a cup of coffee and take my omelet to the table. The guys grab theirs and all disappear, but not Phoenix. He joins me at the table.

"Thanks again for this," he says seriously, pointing at his food. "That was very thoughtful. I know you weren't too happy with me earlier."

"It's fine, Phoenix. I should have locked the door. That was my fault."

"Yeah. You did leave it half open like I did yesterday." He laughs.

"The house was quiet, so I thought everyone was gone. Both days." I laugh once I realize I fell for the same shit two days in a row.

"See. Easy fix. We both just need to lock the door when we're in there," he suggests.

"Agreed."

"I AM CURIOUS ABOUT SOMETHING, THOUGH," HE continues. *Here we go.* I knew it was coming. "Why all the makeup? You are so beautiful without it. And those curves, just wow. That petite waist and curvaceous ass. It's a shame to cover all that up with those baggy clothes you wear."

I slap his arm, not so softly this time. "Shut up, Phoenix. You didn't see shit. And I wear the makeup because I like it."

"I call bullshit. You're hiding behind a persona you've created. You're not Goth. I know people who are, and you're not it," he accuses.

"Who the fuck said I was Goth or even trying to be? You all assumed that. I just happen to like black and baggy clothes. Get the fuck off my case. It's none of your damn business." I push the plate away from me because I've lost my appetite.

"I just about have you pegged, princess. I know hurting when I see it. Don't worry, I don't plan to pry because it is your fucking business. Why would I give a shit? Oh, and I saw plenty with your naked ass pressed against the reflective glass. I saw the curves of your breasts too with that pitiful excuse for a towel you were holding up—such a waste."

I'm so spitting mad that I'm speechless. He doesn't wait for my retort. He pushes his plate away, and the chair screeches against the tile as he gets up. "A fucking waste," he mumbles again as he walks off toward the first floor.

"Stop trying to figure me out, asshole," I finally get out when he is halfway down the stairs.

"Already have," he retorts. A few moments later, I hear the door slam downstairs. So I guess we're back to square one. One step forward and two steps back. I hope Asher didn't overhear our fight. I don't want to explain that Phoenix saw me half-naked, which was apparently a little more than half, according to him. I get up and gather his plate with mine and toss the remainder of the food in the trash. I rinse the plates and stick them in the dishwasher. I need to talk to Irelyn. I miss her, and I need someone to unleash all this shit on. It's a little after eight in California right now, so she should be up. Still, I text her, just in case she is not alone.

Me: Call me if you can. No rush if you have company

A minute doesn't even go by before my phone is ringing. "Hey, Irelyn," I sigh into the phone.

"Nuh-uh, heifer. You wait three days to call me, and then it's when you have issues. Damn, woman, what could possibly be wrong already?"

"Sorry. I was taking time to get settled in, and who says anything is wrong, puta?" Irelyn laughs so hard at me, calling her a whore in Spanish that I have to take the phone away from my ear. This is how we speak to each other, but nobody else better try it.

"I know you, pendejo," she says, continuing with the Spanish insults.

"Miss you already, cray-cray." And I do. I wish she were here with me.

"You already know I was missing you before you even left, Harlow," she says, suddenly serious. "Now, tell me what's wrong."

That is all the prompting I need. I delve into everything that has happened in the past few days. I tell her how Phoenix drives me crazy and how I have unwanted reactions to him. It's like I know better, but I can't control my thoughts about him.

"It sounds like you got it bad, girlfriend. Your mind is saying one thing, but you're right. You can't hide the truth from yourself. I have to say this is the first time I've heard you speak this adamantly about a guy in the two years I've known you. They're the enemy, remember?" Of course Irelyn doesn't know the real truth about why I'm turned off by men, but she respects me enough not to pry. She's always said that when the time comes and I'm ready to share, then I will. Until that day, she won't push. No, I'm not into women either. I love Irelyn, and I'd be willing to share my story with anyone, it would be her, but I can't. If I speak those demons, I fear they will haunt me even more than they already do. No. I choose to suppress those memories to the extent that I'm able. Phoenix is the first guy to get my attention since even before I met Irelyn.

AND WOULDN'T LUCK HAVE IT THAT HE IS TOTALLY unattainable. He is definitely a "hit it and quit it" type of guy. It's better this way, I guess. It helps me keep the promise I made to myself about not letting a man get close to me.

"Yes, I remember, and they still are," I reply. This is why I needed to talk to her. She gives me perspective.

"I need to meet this sexy motherfucker who has succeeded in turning my friend's head," she kids. "I guess I'll see for myself tomorrow." It takes me a second to process what she just said, but when I do, I let out a squeal.

"You're coming here?" I can hardly contain my excitement.

"Yes. Sasha is coming with me. I hope that's okay." Sasha is her cousin that is one year older than us. I don't dislike her, but she is a little snooty. "My aunt went on a cruise for a week. Sasha came to stay with me while she was gone, but I was already planning to surprise you. I told you I was missing you before you left."

"No, that's fine."

"We will be arriving at ten in the morning. I'll call you once we check in to our hotel."

"No way. You're staying here. Let me talk to Asher. You can sleep with me. I'm sure one of the guys can double up." I hope Asher and the guys agree to it. "How long are you staying?"

"Just a few days. I plan to register for classes while I'm there." I forgot about that.

"Great. Let me talk to Asher, and I'll call you this evening. I can't wait to see you."

"Same here." We say our goodbyes, and I try to think about how I'm going to approach Asher. I can usually get my way with him, but I don't know how the guys will feel about it.

CHAPTER SEVEN
Phoenix

I walk into the house, but it's empty. Taking a quick look out at the lake, I see a couple of the guys in a canoe. I see Harlow sitting in one of the chaise lounge chairs fully clothed—meaning the absence of a swimsuit. Isn't she uncomfortable with all of those clothes on? It's August here in the South, so even though it's nearly five in the afternoon, it still quite hot. I set my helmet down and walk down the pier to join her. I sit in a chaise next to hers.

"Hi," I say simply. I know she still might be upset about the fight earlier, so I'm treading carefully. She looks over at me, dumbfounded.

"So that's it? You're just going to pretend you weren't a jackass to me before you left."

"I don't want to fight with you, Harlow. Let's just start again." Her eyebrows knit as if she is puzzled about something, but then she just shrugs.

"Look. I don't have the energy to fight with you, either. I don't want to be the one to come here and cause a rift between everyone. Just keep your eyes to yourself and your nose out of my business, and we will be fine." She's being snarky, but it doesn't bother me. Whatever keeps the peace. I lean my chair all the way back, cross my hands behind my head, and close my eyes. I can feel the sun beaming down on me as the first bead of sweat drips from my forehead.

"Uh, what are you doing?" she questions.

I open one eye and peer over at her. "Sunbathing. What does it look like?"

"But you're in regular clothes," she says.

"So are you," I point out, and she chuckles. I close my eyes and continue my mission to put her at ease. The guys are farther down the lake now, having a good time, and I don't want her to be alone. It's the least I can do—my peace offering. The sun disappears behind the trees, and I'm thankful that I won't be as red as a lobster trying to keep her company. After about ten minutes, she leaves to go back inside, and I'm happy to follow, walking into the house where the A/C is so welcoming. I grab a glass of water while she takes a seat on the sofa. I take my water and go sit next to her.

"What are we watching?"

She looks over at me and smirks. "You're being weird,

but whatever. I watched your show, so you're welcome to watch *Elementary* with me."

"I love that show," I say, a little too excited.

"Sure, you do," she replies in doubt.

"Joan and Sherlock are consultants for the NYPD. She used to be his sober companion, but now she helps him solve all these cool murders." She gives me that same puzzled look she did outside. I need to rein in my sharing.

"So I guess you do watch the show, but it isn't one of your recordings on the DVR," she says, still scrolling.

"Yeah, the guys would probably laugh me out of the house, so it's a secret," I lie. I do watch the show, but I don't record it here. "Besides, if I happen to miss an episode, I can catch it on Hulu. That saves space on the DVR for someone else to record something."

"True," she answers as she ponders that explanation. "Well, did you see the last episode because I'm about to watch the latest one?"

"Sure did. Go for it." She starts the show, and I enjoy trying to guess who the murderer is before she does. It is always the most unlikely suspect. I can't help but sneak glances at her. She is beautiful, even with the shit she has caked on her face. Her laughter is infectious. The guys walk in near the ending of the show, and Asher gives me a look. No words need to be spoken. He is silently warning me off his sister.

When the credits begin to roll, I excuse myself to go

work on the lyrics for "Come Undone," and Asher follows me. I somehow knew he would. "You're not trying to push up on Harlow, are you?" Yup. Straight to the point.

"No, man. Just trying to make her feel welcome. You guys are the ones who left her sitting by herself while you went canoeing." Reverse tactic—a skill unmatched.

"She didn't want to go. Look, you're right. Just checking. She's not like most women. I have to look out for her."

"Of course. And I can tell she's different." I pat him on the shoulder and slide the headphones on to signal the end of our conversation. The truth is, I'm not so sure. I can't say for certain he has nothing to worry about. She is a gazelle right in the midst of a lion's den, so I'm not sure he can protect her from the inevitable. Women are plentiful, yet they don't hold a candle to this one. Harlow has an aura of light that attracts even the worst of demons. I feel the pull, and I know that this is all temporary. I have shit I need to be focusing on, like these lyrics. I turn the track up to "Come Undone" and get lost in the transitions. In no time at all, it all flows seamlessly. I finish the song in about an hour. Before it's even shared, I know this one will be special.

Asher informs us later that Harlow's friend and her friend's cousin are coming into town in the morning and want them to stay here. The guys are a little too quick to agree. This has been a woman-free zone for a reason. I think the idea is asking for trouble, but I'm not going to be the one to reject the idea. Not me of all people. Harlow already took the biggest room, so I'm not sharing the room I'm sleeping in. Asher agrees to share with Killian and open his room to this Sasha chick while Irelyn shares with Harlow. Let's see how this fiasco plays out.

Harlow

I was the first one up and ready to go this morning. Asher is taking me to pick up Irelyn in a few minutes, and I can hardly wait. You'd swear we haven't seen each other in a few years rather than a few days. I've eaten breakfast, made breakfast for the house, including Phoenix's egg white omelet, and now I'm pacing. Asher calls me from downstairs, and I'm already halfway to him before he can tell me he made his room ready for Sasha. My gut turns with the mention of her name, but she will not ruin the visit. I'm curious to see what the guys think of her snooty ass. Surely, Phoenix wouldn't be interested. He is a bit of a diva himself. He's used to receiving attention and being chased, not the other way around, so no worries there. *What the hell am I saying?* I'm not worried either way.

"So you're pretty excited about seeing your friend, Irelyn, huh? Didn't you see her like a few days ago before you left?" I know Asher is teasing me.

"That is ages in girl time, smarty. Seriously though, she needed to come down to register for classes that start in a couple of weeks. She could have done it online, but she wanted to take this time to tour the campus with me."

"Is she a journalism major, too?" I'm not sure if he's truly interested or just making conversation.

"Yes, but her focus is different from mine. She wants to report the news—boring," I joke.

"What about Sasha?"

"Oh, no. She attends UCLA and is an English major. Irelyn and I both know she really just wants to meet some jock and get married so she can be taken care of. She is only attending college for her mother's sake and to find a suitor that fits the bill." Asher laughs at my description of Sasha, but it's the truth. She is a snooty gold digger. I fill him in on how Irelyn and I met when I first started at the community college, and how she refuses to let me be an introvert. We have been like two peas in a pod ever since.

"I like her already then," Asher says. "I think you need to get out even more, so I'm glad she's decided to come down. You guys should do something tonight. The guys and I are planning to grill this afternoon for your guests, but maybe you can find something to get into later. I'm not sure there will be much to do on a Tuesday, but you can see."

"Maybe. I'll check with the girls and find out what they want to do." He knows I'm not much of a partier. Other than Irelyn, I prefer my own company. She knows this too, so she doesn't push. I have my suspicions that she would go out more; if I did, so I hope when we start at the university, she doesn't let me hold her back.

WHEN THE GIRLS GET TO THE CAR, I HUG IRELYN AND halfheartedly do the same to Sasha. The half top has her girls runneth over, and her jeans look painted on, they're so tight. Stilettos complete her look. Yup...same old Sasha. She always dresses to impress or, shall I say, to snag a man. Irelyn, on the other hand, is outfitted in a simple sundress and sandals. I introduce them to Asher, and I notice his gaze lasts a little longer on Sasha. I can't deny that she is gorgeous. She has thick curly brunette hair and green eyes. Her olive skin tone is flawless, courtesy of her Mediterranean roots. As I said, she is beautiful, but her attitude is shitty. I haven't seen her in months, so maybe she has matured some.

Irelyn and I gossip and talk about our favorite television shows the whole way back to the lake house as though Asher isn't in the truck. When we finally park, I'm guessing he is ready to be back with the guys. He announces our arrival when we walk into the house and heads back out to grab Sasha's and Irelyn's luggage. The reactions are all the same. The guys are welcoming, but they zero in on Sasha like fresh meat. Phoenix is the last to join us in the living room. He gives the girls a simple chin tilt and mumbles hello, before taking a seat on the sofa and turning on the TV.

"I'll start the grill," Killian announces. "Asher and I have already purchased some meat this morning if someone wants to season it."

"I'll do it," Ren volunteers.

"I'll help," Irelyn tells Ren. Sasha walks over to the other sofa and sits across from Phoenix. She crosses her legs and runs a hand through her hair. It is obvious to me who she has set her sights on. *Figures.* I join Killian outside to see if I can help.

"Nice friends you have there," Killian says, making small talk as he works with the propane.

"Irelyn is my best friend. Sasha is her cousin."

"So, you aren't friends with Sasha?" He peers over at me.

"I'm not saying that. We're not enemies. I just don't know her that well," I lie. The truth is, I know her and her type too well.

"Yeah, well, it looks like she isn't wasting any time getting to know Phoenix." He chuckles. I look through the glass into the living room. Sasha is now sitting right next to Phoenix, and they're talking. "He'll probably hit that before morning."

"Probably," I agree. A lump forms in my throat at the thought. Dammit, why should I care? I don't want him. Killian and Irelyn come outside with seasoned chicken, fish, and sausage, and I'm happy for the distraction. Asher is right behind them with a cooler. Sasha and Phoenix finally decide to join us outside on the deck. With a click of a remote, Asher starts some music. Jeremih's "Planes" begins to play.

HEINEKEN BEERS ARE PASSED AROUND. THE GUYS START to sing the lyrics and have a good time. Sasha sways her hips to the beat, and I swear every eye is glued to her ass, including Phoenix's. She always gets all the attention. She knows exactly what she is doing.

"Why don't you ladies change into swimsuits, so we can take this party down to the lake?" Phoenix suggests. I'm sure he is just anxious to see Sasha, in particular, half-naked because he knows I'm not going to wear a swimsuit.

"Sounds like a great idea," Sasha replies. She pulls on Irelyn's arm. Irelyn looks over at me, unsure. She knows that I won't change.

"Go ahead. I'll be here when you get back. Third floor, master bedroom to the right." Asher adds that he already put both of their things in there for now.

"You're not going to change?" Phoenix winks at me,

and I roll my eyes. I don't even entertain his question. I walk off, leaving him standing there and head down the stairs, leading to the chaise lounges by the lake. I down my beer in a few gulps. The guys disappeared to change into their board shorts, so it looks like I get to be the oddball in my usual dress of baggy jeans and T-shirt. Irelyn and Sasha are the first to meet me by the lake. Irelyn brought another beer for me. Sasha's micro thong bikini doesn't leave anything to the imagination. Talk about thirsty.

I look over at Irelyn in exasperation, and she mouths, "I know."

Sasha waits until the guys all arrive to flaunt her assets. "Phoenix, do you mind passing me another beer?"

"Sure, doll." He smiles. He passes her the beer, and flirtation between the two of them is blatantly obvious as he brushes his fingers across hers. I want to puke.

"Harlow, aren't you uncomfortable with all those clothes on? It's only going to get hotter, you know." Sasha is trying to call me out in front of the guys. They all go quiet to hear my response.

"It's okay. I don't need my tits and ass hanging out for attention. I'm fine, thanks," I snap.

"Damn." Killian chuckles.

"No need to be jealous, Harlow. I just asked a question. You could be fucking naked for all I care." I sit up straighter in my chair, ready to curse this bitch out, but Irelyn puts a hand on my shoulder in a silent plea.

"Whoa," Phoenix interrupts. "Why don't you come take a dip with me, Sasha?" He grabs her by the hand to pull her away, and she doesn't resist. That makes my blood boil even more. She hasn't even been in the house for an hour, and he is taking her side. *Fuck him and her.* Just yesterday, he stayed clothed here with me in that very chair so I wouldn't be alone, and today, he is acting as if I don't matter. I can already see how the girls' visit will play out, and I hate it. As usual, it will be all about Sasha. Even worse, I have to watch her make a play for Phoenix, and he allows it.

CHAPTER EIGHT

Phoenix

Sasha is giving me all signs that she wants to fuck me. She sat across from me when she first arrived, waiting for me to make a move. She knows she's hot. I'm sure men usually trip over themselves for her, but I don't chase. I waited for her to come to me, and as expected, she did. She led with small talk, but her body language and her constant excuses to touch me gave her away. Harlow is beside herself with jealousy, but she will never admit it. She hates that someone else has my attention. The eye rolls and silent treatment all indicate that she doesn't like Sasha or the time I'm spending with her. Sasha was out of line for calling Harlow out on her decision not to change like everyone else. I've separated the two women, so shit doesn't escalate. We're here in the lake for a swim, and Sasha has her legs wrapped around mine. My cock has a mind of its own, and right now, it wants to come out to play. Not now, though. I grab her ass under the water and give it a squeeze. In response, she rubs her pussy against my crotch. *Just as I thought.*

"So hard," Sasha whispers.

"Your pussy is rubbing against my dick. What did you think would happen?"

"I think we should take this inside. You can go first, and I'll follow."

"Meh. Maybe later, if I decide that is what I want." One thing she will have to understand real quick is that pussy is a dime a dozen. Just because you can make my dick hard doesn't mean I will share. I'll decide as the day progresses if she is worth my time.

"Okay," she agrees. She doesn't argue. Smart girl. A point in her favor. I rub my index finger across her slit before smacking her ass.

"Let's get back to the group," I tell her. When we get back on the deck, Harlow is even more distant. She refuses to look at me now. It seems she needs to understand as well—I don't chase. Me being nice to her a few times doesn't give her the upper hand. If she wants to look down her nose at me, I will give her a reason. She just solidified her fate. I know that she is jealous, and I'm going to push those buttons. I will be fucking Sasha tonight, and I will make sure she finds out. If she wants to keep pretending that she doesn't want me, she can continue playing that game by herself. She can watch as other women get what she is too afraid to act on. Too bad for her. Maybe a good fucking would have brought down those walls she is so desperately trying to hide behind.

"Sure," Sasha says, bringing me back to the present. As she walks up the stairs to the deck, I make it obvious that I'm looking at her ass.

∼

As the day turns to evening, we all gather on the top deck around the firepit. The air is a little cooler, and I think we all have a buzz. We've enjoyed delicious food. I've fucked off my diet for today.

Sasha is now sitting on my lap, and it is no question to the group whose bed she will be in tonight. Harlow has not spoken one word to me. She has been either quiet or talked to Irelyn. As it gets later, Sasha requests to hear one of our songs. Before I can respond, Harlow gets up and bids everyone a good night. She tells Irelyn to stay, and she will see her in the morning. I can see the concern etched in her friend's face, but in the end, she stays put. I deny Sasha's request and tell her she will have to just wait and come see our performance at the bar Friday. We only hang out for maybe another hour before we decide to call it a night. I grab Sasha by the hand and bring her upstairs to my room. It's been a while since I've let my demons out to play, but tonight, I will introduce them to Sasha. She wanted to fuck, so she will get a chance to see what that entails. I don't share these tendencies with my groupies. No, they only get a taste of what I'm capable of. As I said, it's been a while. Normally, I curb my domineering appetite, but tonight, I don't have the inclination to do so. I'm not a Dom in the formal sense of the term, but my taste for control can be extreme.

As soon as my door closes behind her, my alter ego emerges. "My room. My rules. I'm in control," I state as a warning. "Any objections to this, you should leave now."

"No. I understand."

"If at any time you feel uncomfortable or don't want something, simply say stop. I only warn that you be sure you want me to stop because once that word is used, our time together ends. I'm not into persuasion or force." I give her another chance to run the hell out of here, but she only smiles and nods her acceptance of my terms. "Take everything off—slowly."

I watch as she removes her sundress and then that scrap of material she calls a swimsuit. Her immediate and complete submission already has me hard as a rock. Once she is naked, I tell her to kneel before me, and she does again without hesitation. I release my dick from my shorts, and her eyes widen with anticipation. I rub the tip across her lips and tell her to open. She takes me to the back of her throat like a pro and works me with one of her hands. This is what I need. Tonight, I will not think about Harlow. Sasha is in for a night she will not soon forget. I rarely give it my all, but I don't know how long it will be before I find someone else worthy—someone else who can handle what I'm about to unleash. I hope she is ready for a long night. She has willingly given me her submission, and for that, she will be rewarded with incredible pleasure. Tonight, my darkness will prevail, and my demons will play.

Harlow

I awake to Irelyn shaking me. I pull my phone off the nightstand and see that it is already almost nine.

"Get up, girl. It's time to go register for classes." She is already dressed. How is it that she went to bed after me and is up before me? I know firsthand that the two-hour time difference from California is tiring. Well, I had my shower last night, so I only need a few minutes to freshen up. I throw on my usual attire and brush my hair back into a ponytail. This is progress for me because I used to hide behind my hair—the whole purpose I let it grow to my waist.

Once we're out the door, Irelyn stops at the bedroom door next to ours and knocks—Phoenix's room.

"What are you doing?" I hiss.

"Sasha is not in her room. She never made it there, so

I know she's in here," she says apologetically. "I have to let her know we're leaving, in case she wants to tag along." Irelyn is aware of the ambivalence I feel toward Phoenix. I know she hates that her whore of a cousin slept with him. It's for the best, actually. I don't want to see Sasha gloat, though, so I'll just wait for her downstairs. The door swings open, and Sasha stands there with a lazy smile of satisfaction and bedhead. She is wearing one of Phoenix's shirts. Being a glutton for punishment, I see him rise from the bed, covered only by a sheet, to see who is at the door.

"What do you girls want?" Sasha finally asks.

"We're heading to the university. I wanted to know if you were staying or going?" Irelyn asks, frustrated.

"No. I think I'm up for another round with Phoenix. That sounds much more exciting if you know what I mean." She looks back at him and then directly at me.

"Come on, Irelyn. I'm hungry," I say to brush off her direct jab. I keep telling myself I don't care, so why does the ache in my heart from last night seem to be magnified? She says something to Sasha that I can't hear before following me. Asher is letting me take the Escalade. It is about an hour's drive to Tuscaloosa. Irelyn spends the first part of the drive trying to apologize for her slutty cousin and trying to assess how I'm feeling, but I wave her off. I don't want to talk about it. It's not her fault. I have no claim to Phoenix, so he can do what he wants.

I'm not even supposed to like him. My heart tells me I do anyway, but fuck that traitor. It's only because he was the first man to bypass the "fuck-off" vibes that I put out and spend time with me anyway. The attention just caused a lapse in judgment, that is all. I'm confusing appreciation with feelings.

Irelyn finally gives up and lets me have my way. She knows how stubborn I can be. We register for twelve credit hours and manage to get two of the four classes together. *Score.* We spend the rest of the day shopping and getting lunch. I even let Irelyn talk me into buying a dress. I don't know if I'll ever wear it, but it felt empowering to step out of my comfort zone for a moment—knowing that I have the strength to do so.

When we walk in, the guys are all sitting in the living room watching *Family Guy*. Surprisingly, Sasha is not sitting next to Phoenix, but instead, messing with her phone at the dining table. We're told that there is lasagna in the oven and invited to have a seat and a beer. I note that Phoenix is not drinking. He looks at me, but I look away. Irelyn takes a seat among the guys after putting our bags away. I excuse myself to head back out and take a walk. I intended to stay close to the house, but the fresh air and deep thoughts take me farther away than anticipated. As the sun begins to set lower in the sky and the hues of orange transition to purple, I know I need to head back. I don't want to be caught on this country road in the dark. I feel a few droplets of water hit my arms, so I walk faster. Within minutes, the sky opens up to a full downpour. *Shit.* There is no need to run now; I'm getting drenched anyway.

THE ROAR OF A MOTORCYCLE ENGINE SOUNDS IN THE distance as a single headlight blinds me. I put my hand over my forehead to get a better view, and I move closer to the side of the road to let it pass. It comes to a screeching halt next to me, and I nearly jump out of my skin. The rider flips the visor of the helmet, and I'm staring in the eyes of Phoenix.

"Get on," he says.

"No, thank you," I reply as I continue walking.

"Goddammit, Harlow. It's pouring out here. Now is not the time to be stubborn." He is agitated, but I don't give a shit. I don't want anything from him.

"I'm not getting on that death machine with you. I'd rather be wet than dead. Why don't you go ask Sasha if she wants a ride?" Oh, that does it. He's fuming now. I don't slow my pace, but I can hear him cursing to himself behind me.

"Stop with the jealous bullshit and just get the hell on, will you?"

"Jealous? You wish, asshole. You and that tramp deserve each other." I start running to get away from him, but I misjudge the added weight of my baggy jeans from the rain and fall face forward. My hands break my fall, but I'm more than a little humiliated. Phoenix is off the bike in an instant.

He kneels at my side. "Are you okay?"

"Just leave me alone, please." I try to jerk away, but he pulls me into his embrace, and I can't overpower him.

"Please, just stop. Let me get you home safely, and then you can go back to hating my guts. I'm not going to leave you here." I know he isn't lying. I'm learning that he is just as stubborn as I am. We're two fools in the rain, refusing to give in to the other. *Fuck it.* As he said, I can go back to hating him once we get back to the house. I let him help me up.

"Fine. Let's go," I huff. He takes off his helmet and puts it on my head before I can protest. He straddles the bike and then holds it steady while I get on. I'm scared shitless as he takes off. I wrap my arms around his waist tightly and lean with him around each curve. I can feel the hardness of his abs underneath my fingers contract when he moves and the vibration of the seat between my legs. I can admit he handles the bike with expert precision, but that doesn't mean I would want to be on one again anytime soon. When we arrive back at the house, I can't wait to jump off. Asher is standing in the doorway with a scowl.

"I'm glad Phoenix found you. I looked around the

house for you. When it started to rain, I was really worried. Why did you just take off?"

"I just wanted to go for a walk. It's kind of my thing. I didn't realize how far I'd gone, and I didn't know it would rain all of a sudden." I know he was worried. "Sorry for making you worry. It won't happen again. I'll tell you next time I decide to go for a walk." Phoenix walks past us and into the house.

"Irelyn is upstairs waiting on you. She was worried too," Asher continues. She runs up to me and hugs me as soon as she sees me.

"What the heck did you think happened to me? It's just a little rain."

"I don't trust these country woods. You could've been picked up by an ax murderer or something." She giggles, finally at ease.

"Shut up, cray-cray. Nobody wants me."

"That's not true," she says, shoving my arm.

"I'm going to take a hot shower and get out of these wet clothes."

"Phoenix already headed that way. He may have beat you to it," Sasha warns. I'm not talking to this skanky, guy stealing whore.

"You can use the shower on the first floor," Asher offers.

"Go ahead, and I'll bring you a change of clothes," Irelyn chimes in.

"Okay. Thanks." I use the shower downstairs. It is nowhere near as nice as the one in the master bath. I almost feel guilty. I hear the door creak open, and I can make out Irelyn laying clothes on the counter for me.

"I'll just take these wet clothes and put them in the wash," she says, before heading back out the door.

CHAPTER NINE

Harlow

I step out of the shower and immediately notice those clothes are not my things. I run over to them and lift them up. They're some sort of tights and tank with a sports bra. The panties are the only thing that belongs to me. I dry off quickly, wrap the towel around me, and crack the door open.

"Irelyn!" I scream. "Irelyn!" I keep yelling her name until she brings her smart ass down these stairs to see what I want. She knows why I'm calling her.

"Yesssss," she drags out when she gets to me.

"Don't yes me. These are not my clothes. Where's my stuff?" I don't have much. She pushes past me and closes the bathroom door behind us.

"I put all your shit in the wash, so they're wet. This is a goddamn intervention. I'm sorry, but you're just going to have to be pissed with me." I begin to have a mini panic attack.

"Why would you do this? *God.* Now, I need to get something to wear from Asher." I'm so upset with her as I pace the floor.

"Would you listen to yourself? It's fucking clothes, Harlow. It's time to fucking stop hiding behind the damn clothes and makeup. Whatever happened in your past, let it go." She attempts to lower her voice. "You are a strong, independent woman. You don't need clothes to define who you are. I don't know what happened, and you don't have to tell me, but I know the whole point is to make yourself visually unappealing."

"You don't know shit." Tears spill from my eyes, and I angrily wipe them away. How dare she? She yanks my arm and pulls me in front of the mirror.

"News flash, baby girl. You're beautiful no matter what you wear. If you're not interested in the attention of a man, then tell them to back the fuck off. You're feisty as fuck, so I know that you're capable." She breathes out a calming breath. "Those clothes you wear are for a fucking coward, and you are not that. Embrace your curves and sexiness. If you don't want a relationship with a man, you don't have to. This fall starts a new chapter for us, and I will not let you hide anymore. You have me. Just please, give up this whole baggy look. We can go shopping and do girly shit together. And for the love of all things holy, please see that I'm doing this out of love."

I walk over to the tub and take a seat on the edge. Of

all the previous lectures I've gotten from my mom and other people about how I dress, this is the first time that someone has gotten through. I have given power to my past. It's held me captive and made me scared to be seen by the opposite sex. I didn't want to be on their radar. I'm still afraid. It seems silly when you say it out loud, but the clothes and makeup make me feel safe.

THE TRUTH IS, PHOENIX IGNORED IT ALL ANYWAY, AND I'm able to handle him—sort of. He is the ultimate alpha male, so if I can interact with him, maybe I don't have to be afraid of men. This is a big step for me, but I'm going to try. It's better to do a trial run here than on a campus with thousands. Plus, I have Asher and Irelyn here. Jesus, the fact that I'm having this inner monologue with myself about clothes makes me certifiable. I look up at Irelyn, and she gives me the brightest smile imaginable. She knows that she has gotten through. She doesn't say anything. She just hands me the clothes. I don't even ask her to leave. She's seen me naked before. The leggings slash tights, whatever the hell you call them, are knee-length, but the tank doesn't cover my ass. I know I'm curvy, and right now, they're all on display. I timidly walk out behind Irelyn up to the second floor.

"Eat your heart out, Sasha." She laughs.

"Ugh," I groan.

"What? Her body doesn't hold a candle to yours, babe. She had shit to say about you not changing into a swimsuit yesterday. She is going to wish you were still hidden. The guys are going to flip their shit, so be ready. This is your test."

"Thanks." Now I dread going upstairs even more. I'm not going to back out now, but I pray they don't make too much of a big deal over my transformation.

"What the...?" The question dies on Ren's lips. The guys all turn to see what got him so excited.

"Well, I'll be goddamned," Phoenix says. "There she is." He walks over to me and shakes my hand before I can yank my hand away. "Hi, Harlow. Nice to finally meet you."

"Cut the shit, Phoenix," I chastise.

"I don't see what the fuss is about. So she finally put on some normal people clothes and washed all that shit from her face," Sasha whines. "Good for you, Harlow."

"Fuck you." I'm tired of her shit, so I give her the middle finger. Asher steps in to defuse the tension.

"I like it, sis. You don't need all that baggy shit. You're a beautiful woman, not some Goth or tomboy."

"Can everyone please stop focusing on me, please? Don't make this weird for me. It's something I'm trying to see if I like it. Everyone has their own personal style, so get off my case."

"Anyone want to watch *American Horror Story?*" Phoenix changes the subject. He looks over at me and winks. I still hate that he slept with the skank, but he is not mine, so I can't hold that against him. I do appreciate his effort to take the spotlight off me. It works because the guys begin to grab plates of lasagna and beers to settle in for the show. Phoenix, of course, grabs a plate of chicken breast and greens.

I laugh when Sasha tries to poach on his food, and he tells her no. He says he only has enough for him, but I happen to know he has a fridge full of prepped food. Karma is a bitch. She gave up her ass less than twenty-four hours ago, and now he won't share his food. I do believe vengeance is a dish best served cold.

∽

A week passes, and Irelyn has since gone, taking her slutty cousin with her. Things have returned to normal, but Phoenix has been a little hot and cold. Some days, he can be sweet and considerate, and other days he can be a douche. He offers to watch *Elementary* recordings with me one day, and then another day, he tells me, "Meh, that show is for pussies." One day, he seems to enjoy my company, and the next day, he is entertaining his groupies. I swear, he gives me whiplash. The good thing is I haven't reverted back to the black baggy clothes. I've been wearing mostly jeans and T-shirts still, but they fit. Irelyn couldn't wait to take me to get a few things before she left. It's not as bad as I thought. I'm just glad I have someone like her in my life who cares enough to call me out on my shit. I miss her already, but she needed to go home to get packed because classes start in a week.

Phoenix

I'M ON THE SOFA, KILLING TIME ON THE NIXON WEBSITE looking at watches, when Harlow comes downstairs at a snail's pace. I zero in on her legs that are on display in the cheer shorts she obviously slept in. She is sexy as fuck. I've been at constant half-mast ever since she started showing that banging ass body she had been hiding. She's quite stacked, with a D rack and an ass you could probably set your beer on. The guys have kept their ogling in check, but I know they have thought about what it would be like to fuck her just once. That shy, immature way she has toward men is at odds with the package she comes in. She's not going to be ready for the attention headed her way once she sets foot on the University of Alabama campus. She has no idea how gorgeous she is, yet so down to earth. She is a rare find.

I do note that she is looking a little pale as she gets closer. I watch as she goes to the refrigerator and puts her head against it. I get up to see what is wrong.

"What's wrong, Harlow?"

"I don't know. I just don't feel very well. I'm achy all

over." I feel her head with the back of my hand, and she is burning up.

"You definitely have a fever. What did you come down here to get? I'll get it for you."

She uses her hand to push off the fridge, and I can't help but notice her cleavage push up against her tank as well. God, she is sick, and here I am, checking out her tits.

"I just needed to get something to drink," she replies.

"You need to eat something, too. Go get back in bed, and I'll bring it to you." She looks at me hesitantly but then decides to listen. She heads back the way she came. I set about fixing something I think she will be able to tolerate while sick. I make her oatmeal with a little more water in it than I use for myself so that it has a soupy consistency and will be easier to get down. I make toast and pull out a breakfast tray while I'm waiting for the two slices to pop up in the toaster. Lastly, I add a glass of orange juice to the tray before grabbing some cold and flu medicine we keep in the medicine cabinet downstairs. I don't know what other symptoms she has, but this should take care of them all. I head back to the kitchen to put the remaining shit on the tray and take it to her.

Harlow has already fallen asleep, so I set the tray next to her on the nightstand and shake her gently.

"Wake up, sleepyhead. You need to eat." She rolls over

and looks at me with those beautiful grays, and I feel a twinge of something in my stomach.

I help her sit up and place the breakfast tray on her lap. She gets all misty-eyed and mouths, "Thank you."

"No problem. Here. Take the medicine first," I suggest as I take the two capsules out of the foil packaging for her. I hand them to her, and she swallows them down with the orange juice. She takes a tentative spoonful of the oatmeal, and again, I encourage her to eat. I step into the hallway to make a phone call after I'm satisfied she is doing as she is told.

"Hello?" Sevyn picks up the phone after the first ring. "Phoenix? Where are you, man?"

"Sorry, dude, but there has been a change in plans. I can't meet up with you today to handle that for you. Can you reschedule?" Sevyn and I have an undisclosed arrangement. We help each other at predetermined times, but our individual involvement with said help is kept strictly between us. The guys know he exists, but only by name. They don't know where I spend my time when I leave here.

On the other hand, he knows about the life I have here, and I know of his. Our partnership requires us both to be knowledgeable of each other's personal life so that the arrangement we have in place is not sidelined by surprises. We have to know what timelines are available to us to be beneficial to each other. Nobody outside of the two of us can know about our connection if our arrangement is to work.

"I GUESS I'M GOING TO HAVE TO RESCHEDULE. I WOULD appreciate a little notice next time, though. This makes me look bad." He sighs.

"I didn't know ahead of time. Harlow is sick, and nobody's here to look after her. I don't know where the hell the guys are. They were gone when I got up." I'm prepared for teasing since I don't normally give two shits about anyone but myself, according to him. Instead, he lets me off the hook.

"Fine. I'll text you later with a new date and time." We hang up, and I see that Harlow has fallen asleep again, this time with the tray still in her lap. She finished the orange juice, at least. I walk over and collect everything to take back to the kitchen. I'm tempted to slide into the bed next to her, but with how on edge I've been, I don't know if I could maintain my control at that proximity. I'm not a saint. She tempts me like no other. Sometimes I feel like she is wearing me down and not the other way around. The fact that I fucked Sasha set us back tremendously. Although I backed out of giving Sasha the whole Dom experience, I still gave her multiple orgasms. That night with her was gratifying at the moment, but I hate the rift it's caused between Harlow and me. I know that she likes me; her jealousy proved that. The crazy thing is, I now feel that it goes beyond the sexual attraction I picked up on initially. Imagine that. Someone wants me for more than just my dick, yet we both continue to participate in this orchestrated dance where we ignore and avoid the inevitable.

Be that as it may, I still have needs right now. I need something tight I can slip in and out of, and then carry on about my business, but I can't leave Harlow here alone to fend for herself. I almost consider the possibility of rubbing one out, although I haven't done that in ages, when I hear the guys coming in downstairs. *Thank fuck.*

"Where in the hell have you guys been?" I ask. I noticed that Asher is not with them.

"Ren and I went to visit the deep throat twins." Killian grins. "Damn, those women have skills." Ren nods his head in agreement.

"Don't get caught up, fellas. Knocking on the same door too many times leads to someone catching feelings and shit." I personally have a three fucks and you're out rule. And that's only if her shit is phenomenal. Basic bitches get the standard one-night stand. If any of them knew the restraint of my actual desires, they'd probably run. Then again, some would be foolish enough to stay and accept all the darkness I unleash, just to have a piece of me. I have to be mindful of the weak. I require submission, not a pushover.

"They know the score," Ren assures, interrupting my thoughts.

"Okay. If you say so." They've been warned. Most women, even the whores, tend to have feelings that have a direct line to their pussies. Play with it too much, and then the heart gets involved. *No, thank you.* I quickly fill the guys in on Harlow not feeling well and ask that they let her sleep, but check in on her. I'll be back in about a couple of hours—right after I get a nut of my own. This makes encounter number three for Rita, so this will be our last fuck. I'll make it a good one.

CHAPTER TEN

Harlow

I've been on campus for about a month, and I'm settling in fine. The adjustment is easy when nobody knows about your past reputation at your other school as the campus weirdo. I just chose to keep to myself and let them assume whatever they wanted from my appearance. Irelyn was the social butterfly and the personality for us both. I know the parties I did get invited to were so that she would agree to go. I didn't go to many, but I did attend a few. Now that I dress like "normal" people for the most part, I fit in with them. This is a new start for me. I'm determined to be more open-minded. I've seen some slutty-look-at-me-I-need-attention women here, but that is to be expected anywhere you go. Some people are just not happy in their own skin. I can attest to this firsthand. They're just on the extreme ends of the spectrum. They underdress, whereas I always used to overdress. Same difference.

Funny how people are willing to accept my introvert nature now since I look like them.

I finish packing my mini suitcase for a weekend stay at the lake house. Irelyn is going away to Atlanta for the weekend with one of our roommates and a couple of other girls from our mutual class. I wasn't up for a wild weekend of clubbing and drinking. I didn't want her to back out of going, so I convinced her that I missed Asher and was looking forward to spending some time with him.

It wasn't a complete lie. I've only been to see the guys twice since school started. However, a small part of me is excited to see Phoenix, too. Our friendship was just starting to blossom when I left. He finally let down his guard a bit, to show the considerate and caring human being that he can be in addition to his whorish ways. It's a part of who he is, but he is single for all intents and purposes. I have my suspicions that things would be different if he had a woman he cared about in his life. He was so attentive to me when I was sick. He showed me a carefree side that I'm sure no other woman has seen in quite some time. I push the excitement that is starting to bubble up inside me aside and wheel my luggage toward the door. Asher instructed me to be waiting on the steps at 4:00 p.m., so he didn't have to come up. He said he would call if he were running late. It's a few minutes till four now, so I hurry to get outside. I drop the handle to my suitcase when I see Phoenix sitting on his motorcycle with his helmet tucked under his arm. When he sees me, he places the helmet on the seat and walks toward me with so much swag I have to keep my jaw from dropping.

Fuck me; I forgot how sexy he is. Okay, not really, but damn.

I LOVE HOW HIS JEANS ALWAYS HUG HIS MUSCULAR thighs, but the fitted hunter green Henley shirt he's wearing shows off his arms, pecs, and abs—oh, my. He has gotten thicker with more muscle. Any woman would die to get lost in those arms. I bet his cuddle game would be strong if he actually cuddled. Somehow, I don't think that's his forte.

"Well, hello, stranger," he cheeses. "Surprise. I told Asher I wanted to pick you up. It would give me a chance to open my baby up on the highway. It's been a while," he mentions, gesturing toward his bike.

"Geez, and he went for that?" Now that the blood is flowing where it's supposed to—instead of to my lady parts—I remember my fear of the death machine.

"Let's just say it took some convincing." He chuckles. "I promised I would be extra careful." He winks, and it softens my resolve. I use to hate that winking crap, but I guess it's growing on me.

"Uh-huh." I fold my arms, but he unfolds them, then waves to someone behind me. I turn to see we have a small audience. Of course, he's a woman magnet.

"Come on. We need to get you another bag for your

things. Unfortunately, that won't fit," he says, already picking up my luggage. "Lead the way." He strolls right past the ogling women without giving them a second look.

"You'll have to wait here." Parham Hall is an all-female dorm. He isn't allowed to come up to the room. I explain this to him, and he is okay to wait in the community living room.

I KNOW HE IS WAITING, SO I EMPTY MY BACKPACK AND shove a few days' worth of clothes, undergarments, and toiletries in it. I left some stuff at the lake house, so this should be enough. I turn to leave, and a girl by the name of Caroline is standing in the doorway. She is usually quiet and prefers to be tucked away with a book, much like myself.

"Who's the guy, Harlow?" She wiggles her eyebrows, and it cracks me up.

"Just a friend," I insist. She gives me the "yeah, sure" look. "He is picking me up for my brother."

"Mm-hmm. I saw the way he looked at you, but if you say so. Hurry and get down there before those women attack your 'friend,'" she says with air quotes. Phoenix couldn't be happier to see me. He grabs the backpack from me and says goodbye to the ladies, who had followed him in. When we're out of eyesight, he makes it a point to tear up a number one of the girls had slipped him. He puts the backpack on my back and tightens the straps. He

PHOENIX RISING: ISSUE #1

grabs the helmet off the seat and puts it on my head. I hate that he won't be wearing one. God. Let's hope it is a nonissue. He gets on the motorcycle before helping me slide on behind him.

"Remember to lean into the turns with me, like you did last time, okay? And hold on tight. This ride is going to get up to speeds much faster than the last time you were on here."

YEAH, THAT LITTLE LAST-MINUTE DISCLAIMER MAKES ME feel wonderful. "I feel so much better now. Thanks," I say sarcastically.

"I gotchu," he promises. He kick-starts, and the engine roars to life. I can feel that familiar hum between my legs again. I lean forward and gladly wrap my arms around his waist. I can feel the diligence of his workout regimen through the six-pack I have the pleasure of holding onto right now. This is the best part. We take off, and I rest my head against his back. I can feel his back muscles as he wields this bike so effortlessly down the road. When we get up to the speeds he was speaking of, I bite my lip, but then I relax and melt into him. I don't know how fast we're going right now, but we're whipping by cars. I snuggle further into him—believing that, as he said, he has me.

In no time at all, we're pulling into the parking lot of a restaurant by the name of Bottega Cafe.

"You like Italian?" Is he kidding me? I pull the helmet

off my head to get a better look at the beautiful architecture of this place.

"It's my favorite cuisine," I admit. "I don't have much money on me, though. How much will this place hit me for? Sorry, poor college student here."

"Nothing because it's on me." I open my mouth to argue, but he puts a single finger to my lips. "Hush. No arguing. The guys may have left the house already for tonight's gig, so there won't be anyone around to cook. This saves time."

I COMPLETELY FORGOT TONIGHT WAS THE NIGHT THEY have a gig over at Club Luxe bar. And still, he volunteered to come get me. He definitely earns brownie points for that. He helps me off the bike and secures the helmet.

"What kind of bike is this?" It's not like I know anything about bikes, so I don't know why I'm asking.

"It's a Ducati Multistrada 1200 S," he replies. The smile he sports tells me he knows I don't know what the shit that is. "Let's eat, woman. You're going to love it here."

For the sake of time, we forego any of the fancy-schmancy main courses and go for the pizza. Gosh, even those are fancy. He orders the Scottish smoked salmon one, and I opt for the white pie with fennel sausage, onion, ricotta, and provolone. It was his idea to get two different ones so that we can share. It's more pizza than either one of us can eat, so it's too bad we can't take the rest to go. They're both too good not to, but we can't take it on the bike. We pair the pizzas with a Riesling, and it goes well together. He limits himself to one glass since he is driving and has a gig, but they're not carding me, so I have a second.

"This is not part of your diet, mister," I tease.

"Oh, I know. I splurge on occasion, and what better timing than with you?" He winks. It may be the wine, but I'm feeling bold.

"So is this your idea of a first date?" I ask jokingly. As soon as the words spill from my lips, I realize my mistake. *Shit.* I watch as his eyebrows knit together in confusion before he regains his composure.

"Harlow, I don't date. Fucking is all I'm capable of. I don't do relationships. Please don't misinterpret our time together because I enjoy it. It's refreshingly different to have a woman as a friend, but I can't give you that." He looks down, and I know the moment is ruined. There's a strained tension in the air.

"Lighten up, Phoenix. I was just shitting with you. Don't get all serious on me. I have someone who I'm interested in at the university," I lie. "He's made a few moves, but he's just a little slow. We're supposed to be meeting for coffee next week." Something else passes over his face, but it vanishes too quickly for me to identify. I hope he doesn't ask any questions about this guy I just made up because he is a figment of my imagination. Thankfully, he lets it go.

"Well, good. You deserve a good guy. As long as we're on the same page." He raises his hand for the check. When he doesn't ask for to-go boxes, I remember we're on the bike and can't take the leftovers with us. It's such a shame to waste so much food, but I'm beyond stuffed.

Although I tried to smooth my dumbass question over as a joke, I still feel some awkwardness between us now.

When we get back to the lake house, he disappears to get ready for his gig. As he thought, the other guys have already left. I debate if I should just stay here until they get back. That decision is soon made for me when Phoenix sticks his head in the door.

"Ready?" So he just changed shirts, some graphic tee. He doesn't say anything else, so I follow him. When we get to the bike, I have the routine down. He puts the helmet on my head, and I get on. The ride is much like my walks. It gives you a chance to think. I don't want to analyze why I asked that question. Do I want something more with him? I've seen another woman hanging off his dick for God's sake, and I'm still subconsciously entertaining the thought of an "us." Well, that idea has been shot to hell tonight. He was honest about what he has to offer, and I have to respect that. He is not trying to run a game on me to get in my pants. The real question is, is it enough? Can I give myself to him for one night and let it be just that—a chance to feel what all the fuss is about. Could things go back to the way they were afterward? Unlike his other one-night stands, there will be no getting rid of me. I'm his bandmate's sister. I will always be around. Not to mention, Asher would kick both of our asses if he knew I was even rolling around the idea.

ONE THING IS FOR CERTAIN. I'M FINALLY AT A POINT IN my life when I'm ready to face my demons head-on. I'm ready to take back my sexuality and not let my past define me. I want to have intimacy without fear of being inept. It may not be with Phoenix, but at least I'm ready for that first step.

~

I TAKE A SEAT CLOSER TO CENTER STAGE THIS TIME AS the guys begin to come out on stage. Tonight's show is a good one. I kick back a few beers and get lost in the vibe of the show. They keep the crowd guessing with various covers—fast and slow tempo. They perform this one song that includes what I call dirty vocals. I've never heard Phoenix's voice this raw. It involves screaming, but then it's right back into silkiness. This alternating mix up of voice control continues as the guys kill "Love. Sex. Riot" by Issues. The women absolutely lose their damn minds. The louder they scream, the more Phoenix turns up the flirtation with them. He takes off his shirt and throws it into the crowd of manic women. I watch a catfight nearly break out to be the one who comes up with it. Sweat glistens from his abs. I can't watch as he comes close enough to the edge to let some big-bosomed woman get a feel of them. She's definitely hot and more his speed. Fuck, what was I even thinking?

Got the message, Phoenix. If this little extra performance is for me, I get it. I don't need to be hit over the head with a visual. Why settle for one mediocre girl with intimacy issues when you can have your pick of any of these women who are not only gorgeous but also secure with their sexuality. No doubts that they could get him off. *Ugh.* Suddenly, I don't want to be here. I remember that they parked the Escalade out back to pack up after the show, so I head that way. Fortunately, it's the same security guy from last time, and he lets me through without hesitation. I walk the narrow hallway and bypass the rooms. I don't even want to think about that visual either, so I head straight out the back door. I see the truck, but nobody is back here, so I can't get in. I didn't think this through but fuck it. I needed to get out of there. The self-sabotaging thoughts that I try so hard to suppress are winning. I said I would never let anyone make me feel inadequate again, and I failed.

I slide down and sit on the ground next to the passenger side of the truck. I don't know how much of a show they have left, but I have no choice but to wait. I should have followed my first decision and just stayed at the lake house. In hindsight, I should have just stayed at the dorms. Irelyn didn't have to know I never made it here. Maybe I can find an excuse to leave tomorrow and abort the whole staying the weekend idea. I don't think I want to come to any more of their shows. I have the gist of what I need in that aspect for my journalism. Why suffer through the pains of knowing I can never measure up to those women he lusts after while on stage?

CHAPTER ELEVEN

Phoenix

Our last song can't wrap up quickly enough. Where the fuck did Harlow run off to? I know I pushed a little harder with the flirtation tonight, but I needed to reinforce what I said earlier. I feel things are changing, and I don't want to blur the lines with expectations. As soon as we finish the last of our set, I head straight to the back rooms, but they're all empty. I know I saw her come this way. Albert, the security guy, comes leisurely strolling toward the back. I know he gets his share of sexual favors from women trying to get to us through him.

"Albert, have you seen Harlow?" I question.

"Who?" I don't have time for twenty questions with him.

"Asher's sister. I saw her come back here." I'm getting frustrated.

"Oh, yeah. She headed to the truck out back." He says

this like that is the most plausible thing to do at this time of night.

"She doesn't have the fucking key to get in the truck. You didn't think to check on her or at least send someone else? Goddammit, Albert."

"Hey. She isn't my priority—" I don't even listen to the rest of his negligent bullshit. I rush out back to make sure Harlow is okay. I find her sitting on the ground next to the tire with her head slumped over her knees. She is asleep. I want to fucking punch something. I'm such an asshole. My heart slams against my chest in a feeling so fucking foreign, it steals my breath.

"What the hell are you doing out here, Harlow?" My presence startles her awake.

"Oh. I got tired of being in there. Thought I'd come out here and wait for you guys to finish." She stands up and wipes the dirt from her jeans like this little stunt is no big deal. Before I know it, I have her pinned against the truck with my body.

"Are you trying to get yourself raped?" She closes her eyes for a split second to hide her emotions from me before delivering a snarky ass comeback.

"Worry about your fans, Phoenix. I can take care of myself," she retorts. "Get off me." Her face is mere inches from mine as I peer down at her; I intake her every breath.

"Make me," I taunt. I want her to see the exact

predicament she put herself in, had I been an attacker. She reaches up and grasps my biceps to shove me, but I don't budge. After a few more unsuccessful tries, she easily gives up. I tilt her chin up to look at me. "See, you're powerless," I say more calmly. She just stares at me, and something in me snaps. I capture her lips with my own. I nip and lick at the seam until she opens for me. And when she does, holy shit. She gives just as good as she gets. The kiss is raw with passion, all pent-up frustrations released. I pick her up and wrap her legs around my waist. I know she can feel the hardness of my dick poking her.

My hands tangle in her hair as I allow myself to get lost in her kiss. Our tongues duel in an epic exchange of lust and need. Her moans have me wanting to take her right here against this fucking truck. I palm one of her tits, and the weight is just right. Through the shirt is nice, but I crave the skin-on-skin contact. I begin to do just that, but we are interrupted by a loud cough.

"What are you doing, man? Asher is looking for you and Harlow. If he catches you like this, he is going to beat your ass to a pulp," Ren warns. Harlow jumps down like a frightened cat. The mention of Asher's name has officially killed the mood. I got carried away. I didn't mean to pounce on her like that, but she sure as shit didn't mind.

"Yeah. Thanks, man." I know this is not the end of this conversation. He is going to have plenty of questions when he gets me alone. Harlow looks down and hurries to the other side of the truck. Ren clicks it to unlock, and she doesn't hesitate to get inside. I walk past him to go back into the bar and let them know I found Harlow while Ren is still standing there flabbergasted. I don't know what to think right now. I want her more than ever, and I won't stop. At some point, this became more than just a challenge to prove I can fuck any woman.

I've been waiting for her to fall at my feet like the rest and beg for the dick. Clearly, that won't come to pass, but it is even more apparent that she wants me just as badly as I want her. We're at a stalemate—a battle of wills. I don't chase, but fuck it. Tonight we took a step toward the inevitable. She wants me, and that is exactly what she's going to get. It's time that I show her what her body craves. She needs a tender and gentle approach, and I'll give her that right before I fuck her world. My dick jumps with excitement for what's about to come.

Harlow

I sit here at a loss for words. That kiss was off the fucking charts intense. I don't know how to feel right now. Phoenix and I can't happen. I was just pissed with his performance in there, for fuck's sake. That being the case, why did every second of that moment feel so right? Animalistic desires are brought to the surface. I could feel his hardness through my jeans, and I wished there was no barrier between us. All of my anger toward him from earlier had dissipated. Maybe "we" can happen if I let go of any expectations for more. For a small window of time, I was able to let go of the pain that usually holds me captive. I wanted this man to devour me.

I didn't care about the skanks in the bar, probably still lined up to get a piece of him. He was with me. He chose me. Maybe we don't need to define what this is and just go with it. I'm deep in thought, replaying our kiss when the guys show up outside carrying their equipment. That was quick. I guess they are foregoing their usual sexcapades that go on after the show. These guys are super talented, and they're only playing gigs for local bars right now. I can only imagine the ass they'll have lined up when they make it to the big stage. I will have to keep this in mind going forward with Phoenix. I can't let my heart get invested. If we give in to temptation, there will be no expectations of a relationship. The sex can be the building blocks I need to reinvent myself and take back my sexuality. Nothing more. Nothing less. Just sex.

During the ride home, the guys discuss how they think the show went with the mix of cover songs. They talk about starting to gradually introduce more of their own material. Phoenix notifies them that he has some record labels he plans to get in touch with. He seems unaffected by tonight's occurrence. I'm anxious to see how he will proceed. Will he pretend it never happened, or will he make the next move? I'd be lying if I didn't say I was hoping for the latter.

~

I DISAPPEAR TO MY ROOM AS SOON AS WE GET BACK TO the lake house, in part because I'm afraid this emotional storm passing through me will read easily on my face. Asher will sense something is wrong. Also, I don't know if Ren told Killian what he walked out on. I don't want things to be awkward. I turn on my night lamp to dimly light the room. I connect my iPhone to my iHome so that I can drown my thoughts out with some Adele. Her latest single, "Hello," plays through the speaker, and I set it to repeat. I love her music. I lay across the bed, getting lost in the sultry lyrics when my bedroom door opens. Phoenix stands there for a few beats before coming in and closing the door behind him. I sit up as my heart slams against my chest. I can see his intent in his eyes.

"Oh, you don't have to get up for what I have in mind," he warns. "If this is not what you want, speak now." I swallow the lump in my throat. I'm speechless. I want all that he is silently offering me. "Okay then," he says with finality. He crawls onto my bed in true predator form. I watch as he pulls his T-shirt over his head. *Sweet baby Jesus...this is really happening.* I tremble slightly at the thought. Phoenix grips my inner thighs before pulling me down closer to him. I lie flat on my back as he undoes the button on my jeans.

I'M THANKFUL THAT I HAVE MY PRETTY BLACK LACE panties on tonight.

"Lift," he commands. His voice is thick, rough, and one of control. He's still Phoenix, but different somehow. I lift my hips as he instructs. He pulls my jeans and panties down with one pull. "Last chance, Harlow. No regrets."

"No regrets," I whisper. That is all the reassurance he needs. He strips my jeans and panties the rest of the way off.

"I can smell how fucking wet you are for me," he says, hovering over me. I cover my eyes with my hands. "No hiding tonight, baby. I'm going to worship this pussy and fulfill all the fantasies you never knew you had," he vows. The vulgar promises he spews make me even wetter. This feeling...this moment... this is how it should be. He sits me up partially, so he can remove my shirt and then my bra. When he has all of my clothes off, I'm naked in every aspect of the word. I hope he knows that I'm giving myself to him in every way—more than just with my body. Though I'm not a virgin, nobody has gotten this far with me consensually. He lays me on my back and brings his body down on top of mine. We're chest to chest, and the heat from the contact is scorching. He gives me a wicked smile before bringing his lips to meet mine. This kiss is so soft. Our tongues slowly meet in a sensual dance that builds the ache between my thighs.

HE PARTS MY LEGS OPEN WITH ONE OF HIS JEAN-CLAD muscular thighs, and I rub myself against him—desperate for the friction. He deepens the kiss while grinding against me. I swear I can come from his kiss and dry humping alone. He nips at my lips and immediately licks away the pain. My body trembles now for a different reason than nerves.

"Hmm. Patience, baby." He plants gentle kisses along my neck before following a trail down to my breast. He gives them each attention with just the right amount of licking and nibbling. So I see he is a nibbler, and it is sexy as fuck. He continues south, and I know where he's heading next. I brace myself as he takes that first lick to my clit.

"Fuuuuuck," I moan. My thighs tighten on their own accord around his head, but he isn't having it.

"Let me in." He pushes my legs apart while simultaneously sucking on my nub. He sucks, then nibbles in a frenzy so enthralling, I feel a sensation of release on the precipice. I grab his hair as I ride the fuck out of his face with wild abandonment. Phoenix is right there with me. He pushes his tongue deep into my entrance and works me toward that orgasm my body so desperately needs. I squirt so hard my whole body shakes. Phoenix looks up at me, so proud of himself. In one quick instant, he rids himself of his jeans. *Damn, he is commando.*

HE TAKES THE CONDOM HE PULLED FROM HIS POCKET and slowly rolls it over his hard cock. He is giving me a show. And oh, what a beautiful cock it is—pink perfection. The length and girth are intimidating, but I will take every inch. I watch as he gives it a few strokes with his hand. "I want your lips around my dick, but right now, I can't wait for a second longer to be inside you," he admits. My legs open as an invitation, and he doesn't hesitate to accept. He positions himself at my entrance and teases me with a few strokes with just the head.

"Stop teasing me," I plead.

"So greedy." He winks. I'm about to object, but then he slams into me, and the words are lost on my tongue. He stills briefly, allowing me to savor his fullness. He stretches me to capacity, and it feels amazing. He eases back and slams into me again. I whimper at the heavenly assault. I claw at his back, so desperate for him to go deeper. He pounds into me a few more times before alternating his thrusts with a slower grind. Meanwhile, Adele continues to be the soundtrack for this fucktastic fucking we're having. I'm already close to the edge again. Just when I can no longer hold off the impending nut, Phoenix changes things up. In one swift move, he flips us so that

I'm on top. He puts his hands behind his head and looks at me expectantly. "My turn, doll."

"What?" I'm guessing he wants me to ride him.

"Fuck me, Harlow. Ride my dick like you own it."

Fuck, I love the dirty talk.

UNSURE OF HOW TO PROCEED, I JUST DO WHAT FEELS good. I sit up until I'm fully mounted. I lift slightly until only the head of his dick is left inside. I alternate sliding completely down his shaft and just the tip. My pussy clenches with each stroke while my tits bounce with the rhythm. His hooded eyes tell me he is enjoying the ride. I'm on fire. I can feel myself dripping down his length. His legs tense underneath me, and his control snaps. He grabs my hips and pushes me down on his dick. He takes over as his hips piston upward to meet mine. He is topping me from the bottom.

"Fuck, I'm going to come," he warns. "Shiiiiiiit," he groans as he finds his release. I can feel the residual twitch of his dick as he throbs inside me. That sensation is enough for me to fall over the edge with him. I throw my head back and come all over him. I then fall forward to rest on him, but he is not done with me. He pulls out of me and tells me to get on my knees. He slaps my ass and pulls off the used condom. He hands me a new one and tells me to hold on to it. He positions himself behind me and nudges the tip of his cock between my ass cheeks.

"Uh, Phoenix," I begin.

"I'm not going to take you here yet, babe." He smacks my ass once again, and the sting makes me wet. "Not tonight, anyway." I don't miss the insinuation of "more." This is not a one-night stand. *Oh, my stars.* He nudges me again, and I can feel him already growing hard again. "I will be taking this sweet pussy from behind, though, so hold on." He takes the condom from me and rolls it down that beautiful gift of his. I look back at him, and his eyes never leave mine as he enters me from behind. He brings me to three more orgasms before the night is over. I'm deliciously sore and looking forward to this "more" that he promises.

CHAPTER TWELVE

Phoenix

Last night was epic. More than I could have possibly anticipated. The guys turned in early, so I decided to continue where I left off with Harlow. She was more than willing. She came beautifully over and over again. Her body responded to mine in every way, and it was fucking perfect. The demons that I hide wanted so desperately to turn things up a notch, but I couldn't let her see that side of me just yet. It would crush me if she ran. For the first time, a woman's openness to my kink matters. She's not replaceable like the groupies. I need to feel her out to see if she can handle my true dominant nature. Is she capable of submitting in the way that I desire? Sure, last night, she followed my lead, and I was in control, but that isn't the same. My tastes are extreme, especially to someone as vanilla as her. She has some underlying issues that I can't quite put my finger on.

I need to go slow until I determine her threshold for submission.

The guys are lounging around the living room this Saturday morning. Ren hasn't said anything to me about what he saw last night, but I know he's waiting to get me alone. I'm playing various Issues' songs with a pep in my step while I'm in the kitchen fixing everyone an omelet—a page out of Harlow's book. Speaking of the vixen herself, I see her coming down the stairs.

She's walking a little slower this morning. I can't help the devious smile that forms on my lips, knowing my dick is the reason for that walk. Feeling mischievous, I switch the song playing to John Legend's "Tonight (Best I Ever Had)." I watch as her face flushes as she picks up on my idea of humor and reference. I sing about being the best she's ever had as she gets closer.

"Stop it," she shushes me.

"Best you've ever had," I repeat in a whisper. I grab her ass as she passes to get to the coffee maker. She nearly jumps out of her skin. "Round two later," I whisper in her ear. I go back to making the omelets, but I relish in the permanent blush she is now wearing. I wish I knew what thoughts inspire that blush.

"Maybe," she replies as she grabs her coffee and hurries past me. She made sure she got the last word in. Oh, there will definitely be a round two, and I will make sure she pays for that little defiance. I was going to wait, but I think I might just have to give her a small taste of what I'm capable of. I have to keep things in perspective. I'm still in control. Her body belongs to me, but she hasn't figured that out yet. I'll just have to help her see it, and it will be my pleasure to do so.

∼

Today, I have to bring Harlow back to school. Yesterday, I wasn't able to deliver on my promise of round two because I was busy with the guys until our gig. We introduced two of our original songs to get feedback from the crowd, so we needed a little more rehearsal time before the show. Harlow decided to stay at the house, which disappointed me because I wanted her response more than anything. I get her reasoning, although she feigned being tired. She didn't want to see me interact with my female fans after we had such a magical night. For that reason, I couldn't be mad. It would have been awkward, to say the least. She was sound asleep by the time we made it in, so I let her rest. The fucking guys insisted that we go sit down and eat somewhere after our gig, so we could discuss how we think it went. It went fantastic, but I couldn't justify a reason to hurry back to the lake house. Now everyone is up again this morning, lounging around the living room. Don't they have some pussy to get into? I need to find a reason to get Harlow away for a few hours before I have to take her back.

"Morning, princess," Asher says with too much excitement for 9:00 a.m. "You missed a hell of a show last night." Harlow comes into the living room and takes a seat next to her brother.

"Sorry. I had some homework I needed to get done before tomorrow, and I was tired." She sneaks a glance at me. "What time did you guys get in last night? I stayed up until one a.m."

"Oh, it had to be well after three," Killian volunteers.

"Hmm. Must have been some night of celebration," she hints as she glances in my direction. I catch the undertones of her insinuation. She thinks we fucked some groupies after our gig. I wasn't even tempted last night. I wanted to get back here and finish what we started.

"Yeah, these knuckleheads wanted to hit up the pizzeria. Fuck my diet," I clarify.

"Yeah, no groupie love last night," Ren jokes, but I know he caught onto the same insinuation that I did. He still doesn't know that the two of us have surpassed just kissing. He is just being the ideal wingman and helping me out. She giggles, so I know everything is okay.

"You and that diet of yours. I don't know how you stick to it while these three eat up everything," she says, pointing at the other guys.

"Hey," Asher says. "Not everything. Besides, Phoenix has the restraint of a saint." If only he knew. Not when it comes to his sister. Ren chokes on the OJ he's drinking. Again we're on the same page. Asher tells Harlow he wants to take her to brunch to spend time with her before she leaves today, and I can see my window of opportunity to spend time with her getting smaller and smaller.

∼

We arrive back at the university just before sunset. As I predicted, Asher spent the entire day with Harlow. She gets off my bike, and I'm disappointed that things didn't work out the way I wanted them to. It's funny, but I'm not ready to say goodbye. She must feel it too.

"You should see the arboretum we have here," she mentions.

"Arbor what?" I question.

"Arboretum," she repeats with a snort. She covers her mouth, embarrassed for a second. "It's like an enchanted forest with trails of mostly tall trees and whatever flowers are still in bloom. It's beautiful, and here on our campus," she continues. I can't say that I really give two shits about this arbor place, but if it means I get a little more time with her, then I'm down.

"Get back on then. Take us to this mystic place," I taunt. That earns me another snort from her. It is so endearing. She hops back on the bike and uses her hand to point in the direction I need to head. We go as far as we can go with the bike and park. I have to say she didn't exaggerate. The oranges and browns of the fall leaves look picture perfect. We walk the trails as she points out various flowers and trees with excitement. I can tell she's been here multiple times. This is not something I would have been interested in, but I admit I'm enjoying this place.

It's so quiet and peaceful. I bet it would be a great place to escape and just write some of our music.

"Isn't this place awesome?" The smile on her face is priceless.

"It is," I answer honestly. She grabs my hand and pulls me until we reach this platform with a canopy view of the forest. "Nice."

"I knew you would like it. You seem like a guy who likes his solitude. This place is so vast; it is easy to get away from it all and just be. I like to come here and think," she admits.

"I bet it would be a great place for other things, too," I hint. She slaps my shoulder in mock exasperation.

"It's only open for maybe another hour. It closes at sundown. No getting your forest freak on," she jokes. "So, I'm sorry I missed your set last night. I really would like to hear some of your original music," she says, suddenly serious.

"I guess you're just going to have to come to our show this coming weekend."

"Oh, I see. I have to wait to hear some with your fans. I'm not special." She looks me in the eyes with those piercing grays. At that moment, I know she has the potential to be dangerous if I'm not careful.

"Well, it's not like I have any music out here," I point out.

"A cappella will be just fine," she assures. I look around, and we're alone. She takes a seat on the wooded platform, so I join her.

I MENTALLY SHUFFLE THROUGH THE SONGS THAT I could possibly share with her, and then I just know. It is a piece that is not yet finished, so this goes against my rules. I don't even share my lyrics with the guys until they're done. They have a chance to participate in any edits or additions after the fact, but the initial concept is always mine alone. The truth is, I've only started it today while Harlow was out with Asher. This song is about her.

"I can share one with you, but it isn't finished."

"Okay," she beams.

"It's titled 'Leave it All Behind.'" I look around one more time to make sure nobody else is around. I blow out a cleansing breath and share a piece of my soul—as personal as it gets for me.

I KEEP TELLING MYSELF IT'S THE LAST TIME
Each time it proves to be a lie
The darkness pulls me deeper into the shadows
It won't let me see the light.

It's a never-ending battle that I can't seem to win,
Maybe one day I'll defeat the devil...
The monster that lives within.

I WANT TO LEAVE IT ALL BEHIND
  I want to leave it all behind
  I want to leave it all behind

TAKE BACK CONTROL... MAKE MY ESCAPE FROM THESE demons I face.
  This is my warning to you.
  This is your chance to be free.
  Don't give in to the hunger I crave
  because I can't be sated.

Harlow

OH. MY. GOD. I'M SPEECHLESS. EVERYTHING ABOUT that song has touched me deeply. Without the music as a distraction, for the first time, I just hear him. The sultriness of his voice is so different from anything I've ever heard him perform on stage or even that day he was practicing with the guys. This is personal. I can feel the pain in those lyrics, a confession of sorts. Someone in his past has hurt him too and may be the reason he has a thing against relationships. I don't want to ruin the moment by prying into his past or the reason for the song, so I don't mention it. Phoenix has such a beautiful voice and I have no doubt in my mind that, coupled with the band's instrumental genius, they will make it far. Tears spill down my cheeks.

"That was so beautiful, Phoenix."

"Yeah? Thank you. I'm sure it will be even better once the guys hear it, and we put it to music." Wait, what?

"You haven't shared this with the band?"

"Nope. You're the first." He stands up and puts his hands in his pockets as he looks around. "I don't normally share my music with anyone, Harlow, until the song is complete. It's a private process. When I'm done, I work closely with the guys to lay tracks to the lyrics that I've written." I'm even more touched now. Whether he realizes it or not, Phoenix just chose to share a part of himself with me that nobody else gets to see.

"Why me?" And what does this mean, but I don't ask that.

"You know, I don't actually know." He shakes his head as if he is trying to figure it out himself. "Maybe because you shared this place with me. It's different. I haven't really spent much time with women outside of fucking. It's nice," he admits. He writes it off as being caught up in the moment of experiencing something different, but I don't believe that. Things are changing between us, and it's not in the direction he intended. He is softly tapping on the brakes, hoping I won't notice—that I won't get offended. *I see what's in your heart, Phoenix. You showed it to me. Someone did a number on you, but that girl is not me.* I wish I could say these things, but I can't since I don't even know what I want. I thought I did, but now I'm not so sure.

"Yeah, maybe." I keep my internal monologue to myself. It's starting to get darker, so I know our time in this bubble has come to an end. They'll be closing soon.

"So when are you coming back to the lake house?" We walk back to the bike, and I'm happy to see my backpack is still there. We left it there since we didn't drop it off at the dorms. Nothing important was in there anyway—just clothes and toiletries.

"I can come down on Saturday. Sorry, I have a study group session on Friday."

"Who in the hell plans a study session on a Friday night?" he jokes. "You need to get a life, babe."

"Ha-ha. Funny. We have a huge history test coming up on Monday. The group opted to meet and study to get it out of the way, so they can party on Saturday and rest on Sunday," I explain.

"Hmm. That makes sense, I guess. Still, studying on a Friday night sucks."

"Yeah, but it has to be done. Anyway, like I said. I can come on Saturday."

"Meh. Don't worry about it. Maybe we can shoot for

the weekend after that." He gets on the motorcycle and hands me the helmet. To say I'm disappointed I won't be seeing him this coming weekend is an understatement. I climb on the back of the bike and grab him around the waist as he takes off. So while I'm fucking studying history this coming weekend, he'll probably be enjoying the company of someone else. By the time I see him again, he will probably have moved on from whatever this is. Maybe it's for the better. No expectations mean no disappointments. And just like that, my mood has turned sour. This is exactly what I didn't want.

I can feel the doubts gnawing at me, telling me I'm not good enough. Why wait for someone who is staying an hour away, when he can have his pick of pussy anytime he wants it? I'm not foolish enough to think I'm that special. There is no question what will transpire next weekend if he even waits that long.

I think I just ripped my own fucking heart out with that reality check, and I don't want him to witness that. When the bike comes to a rolling stop. I quickly thank him for a great weekend and for sharing his song with me before racing into the dorms.

CHAPTER THIRTEEN

Harlow

I awake to Irelyn shaking me. "Get up, woman. You have some explaining to do." What the hell? What time is it?

"It's a little after seven. Now get up." I swear I'm going to murder her. I stayed up and continued studying for that history exam long after everybody wrapped up. I was planning on sleeping in. Irelyn yanks the cover off me and stands at the foot of my bed with her hands on her hips. "You have been holding out on me."

"What?" I asked, puzzled. I try to reach for the cover, but it isn't any use.

"I'm talking about Phoenix. Mr. Hottie-and-I-know-it-and-I-still-fucked-Sasha-Phoenix."

"Can you tell me why you're waking me up so damn early to talk about Phoenix?" What did she hear? Did somebody describe to her the guy who picked me up and dropped me off last weekend and figured out it was him?

"Because he's downstairs in our lobby, that's why."

"What?" Okay, that got my attention. I jump out of bed. "You're lying."

"You little slut. You totally fucked him," Irelyn accuses. "When were you planning to tell me? It was last weekend, wasn't it? When you went to the lake house by yourself."

"Yes. Alright? Keep your voice down." I don't bother lying. Once she gets on something, she is like a dog with a bone. I was going to tell her anyway. We just haven't had much alone time. Right now, I'm more curious to see what Phoenix is doing here.

"Go, woman, but we're going to talk," she chastises. I give my appearance a quick check in the mirror. I pull my hair in a ponytail to tame the bedhead and run to our community bathroom to brush my teeth. It's early, so there is no wait to use it. My tank top and sleep shorts are borderline inappropriate due to my plentiful assets, but he has seen me in less. I give myself one more look over and decide; this will have to do.

When I get downstairs, Phoenix stands there looking like a wet dream. Really, it's unfair that he looks this gorgeous this early in the morning. He is wearing a shirt that says Flex Till You're Famous—No Sleeve Gap and jeans. There are definitely no sleeve gaps around those guns, and the famous part is just a matter of time.

"Morning, beautiful," he says immediately upon seeing me.

"Morning, sexy." I grin. To think I've fretted all week with scenarios of what he would be getting into this weekend, or shall I say whom, and now here he is. "You guys didn't perform at the bar last night?"

"We did," he says cryptically.

"And you still rode an hour out here to come get me, I'm guessing?" Aren't you tired?"

"Meh. I slept enough. And I am here to get you, just not to take you to the lake house." Okay, now I'm confused.

"Oh, no? Where are you taking me?"

"You'll see. Go get dressed. I'm starting by taking you to breakfast."

"Do I need to pack anything?"

"Nope," he answers simply.

"Okay, oh cryptic one," I joke. He laughs and tells me to get a move on. It doesn't take me long to shower and get dressed. I'm not sure where we're going, but he is dressed casually, so I put on jeans and a V-neck shirt. The girls are partially on display. He should get a kick out of that—both because I am actually showing a bit of skin in public and because I think he is a tit man. When I walk back downstairs, he is staring out of the window, deep in thought.

"A penny for your thoughts?" I ask.

"Hmm. You don't want to be in my head, babe. You'd be traumatized by what you find in there." He winks. "Come on. Let's get going."

~

Breakfast is an experience, especially for a broke college student. We had eggs Benedict and mimosas on the terrace of some quaint little restaurant. It sure as hell feels like a date, but I won't ruin the moment with assumptions. I'm waiting to see just what he has planned for us. We spend the next couple of hours taking a walk in the park, having a late lunch, and then finally a visit to an art museum. Phoenix tells me the guys would laugh him out of town if they knew of his appreciation for art. He likes sculptures, too. I agree that everything is so beautiful. One particular painting of a crying woman catches my eye. The pain in her features is evident, but her posturing is at odds with the tears.

I see strength. These are the last tears I will shed type of strength. The associated price tag is unbelievable. It's almost twenty grand. Well, I hope someone else gets it. It's an amazing masterpiece. The day we have shared together can without question be considered a date, but I'm sure he is not classifying it as such. The day flies by, and I hate to see it come to an end. He has another gig tonight in a few hours, so I know he has to leave soon. The drive back will take him an hour. As we head out of the museum and toward his bike, he says what I have been thinking.

"I have to get back, but I have one last surprise for you," Phoenix hints.

"Yeah? What is it?" I ask excitedly.

"It wouldn't be a surprise if I told you, nosy." I cross my arms, but he is not persuaded to give me any details. Instead, we get on his bike and ride for what seems like ages. We finally come to a stop at a boutique-style hotel, and I don't know what to think. So the big surprise is a visit to a hotel. Clearly, he is looking to finish what we started last weekend.

"What a nice surprise," I finally say, mildly intrigued.

"You'll see," he comments while parking. "Come on." When we get inside the hotel, he heads straight toward the concierge, and they discuss his reservation.

"Enjoy the rest of your day, sweets." He winks.

"What do you mean?" *Is he leaving me here?*

"This is George," he responds, pointing at the concierge guy. "He is going to take care of you this afternoon, starting with an hour massage." He smiles, and I just want to kiss his face off.

"What?" I ask again. I just can't believe he is doing this for me. Phoenix is anything but romantic. Not to mention his self-proclaimed aversion to relationships and dating. His actions today are a direct contradiction to his proclamation.

"Swedish massage, facial, pedicure, and manicure, ma'am," George clarifies.

"Yes. What he said." Phoenix grins. "I'll be back after our show tonight. After you're all pampered and relaxed, I'm going to get you all worked up again," he promises.

"I think I like this plan of yours," I agree. I will be ready for him when he gets back.

"Glad to hear it," he admits. "See you later." He turns and leaves, while George tells me to follow him. He escorts me to the hotel spa and introduces me to Hilda. He runs down the list of services that I'm to receive, and she nods her understanding. The experience is amazing. I'm given a place to change out of my clothes and then given some infused water. I'm massaged and polished with Dead Sea mud and seaweed. My skin feels so soft and supple. Now, I'm ready for tonight. A few years ago, I wouldn't have imagined I'd be where I am sexually. Up until this summer, I repelled any man who tried to get close to me.

MY BODY CRAVED PHOENIX FROM THE BEGINNING. I just wasn't willing to listen. After arriving on campus and not having anyone come close to eliciting those feelings, I decided to throw caution to the wind. Tonight, I will do just that.

∼

When Phoenix gets back, it's late. He finds me asleep on the bed wearing nothing but the hotel bathrobe. I'm awakened by him crawling into bed with me and loosening the robe.

"I waited for you," I say groggily. "What time is it?"

"Just after two." He continues to open my robe until I'm bare to him. The room is dark with the exception of the moonlight shining through the sheer curtains, peeking through the blackout drapes. "I had to ditch the guys, and they still wanted to know where I was going."

"Jeez. And you call me nosy. You didn't tell them, did you?"

"Are you kidding me? Are you trying to get me lynched by my balls? Asher would kill me." He chuckles. "No. They think I'm meeting up with some random chick from the show."

"Nice," I say sarcastically. This is just sex, and I know it. So why does a pang of jealousy rip through me that we have to hide what we're doing? The reality is that I'm just a hookup even though I'm not random.

"Get out of your head. It's just something I let them think. My dick was semi-hard all night, thinking about what I had waiting on me."

"Mm-hmm," I say doubtfully.

He hovers over me and leans down until his lips are

mere inches from mine. He licks the seam of my lips, and it's surprisingly erotic. It's his thing. My tongue sneaks out to meet his, and he greedily captures it and deepens the kiss. Our kiss is passionate and sensual. My body comes alive in his arms as he owns me with just his lips. He sits up to pull his shirt off, and the moonlight dances across his abs. A thought crosses my mind, and I decide to run with it. I push my robe off the rest of the way before sitting up on my knees. I tug at his jeans, and my intent is clear. He helps me pull them off. No surprise, he is commando. I just make out his cock, but I don't have to see it in the light to know that it's beautiful. This is huge for me, but I need to taste him. When the jeans are completely off and on the floor, he lays back and puts his hands behind his head. His cock stands proudly as it waits for my attention. I grasp him and bend at the waist to get reacquainted with his engorged dick. I swirl my tongue around the head before taking him deeper. I can feel his legs tense underneath him. He is too big to deep throat to the base, so I use my hand to stroke him while I suck. He's clean-shaven and his dick is so smooth. I can feel my pussy getting wetter every second.

I MOAN AROUND HIS DICK, AND HIS HIPS BUCK.

"Holy fuck," he groans. He grabs my head and begins to push my mouth up and down on him—controlling the tempo. His enthusiasm sparks mine. I roll my tongue along the shaft while massaging his balls. I find the vein on the dorsal side, underneath the tip, and give it a little tongue play. I'm enjoying every inch of his cock. "Baby, I'm about to come," he warns. I stroke him faster and continue sucking him toward his release. He explodes in my mouth, and I still can't find it in me to part with his dick. I refuse to stop as his legs shake, and I swallow every drop. In a flash, he flips me to my back. He expertly fingers me with a vigorous massage to my clit.

"Phoeeeeeenix," I cry out. His fucking fingers are magic. I can only hold on for the ride.

"Come for me, baby. Give it to me." The lust his voice is thick and such a turn-on. His skillful fingers continue their assault until he milks an orgasm from me. "That's it, baby," he encourages. I'm lying here in the afterglow when he buries his face between my thighs to start round two. His tongue is every bit as magical as his fingers. He twirls that talented tongue slowly around my clit, and I can feel the buildup start again. I arch my back as he sucks on it. This man knows exactly the delicious torture he is bringing me.

I GRAB HIS HAIR AS MY OWN LEGS BEGIN TO SHAKE. His tongue delves deeper into my opening as he enjoys me losing control. He inserts a finger and makes the "come here" motion. With the crook of his finger, I come in waves. *Holy shit.*

"Somebody likes that," he teases. I can't even respond because I'm still in an orgasmic trance. "I have so many ways to make you come. It's going to be fun showing you just how," he promises. He reaches for his pants at the end of the bed and slides on the condom he retrieves. I watch in complete fascination at the lengthening of his cock. How could it possibly get any bigger? He strokes it for my viewing pleasure in the dimness of the room. The act itself is erotic foreplay, knowing he is hard because of me. When he gets out of bed, I'm confused. He summons me to join him, so I follow suit. I'm not out of bed fully before he is spinning me around to face it.

"What...?" The question dies on my lips.

"Head down, baby, and ass up." He uses a hand to guide me into the position that he speaks of. I place my hands forward on the bed and bend over; my pussy pools in preparation for him. He slaps my ass a couple of times, and the sting only creates more wetness. "So fucking beautiful," he praises.

I feel him nudging at my folds, and I can hardly stand the wait. He's playing with me.

"Dammit, Phoenix. Can you just fuck me already?"

"Patience, baby. Sometimes getting there is half the fun." He enters me slowly, but just the tip. I try to back up to take more of him, but he stills my hips. "Nuh-uh. My terms. I feel that hungry pussy of yours clenching my dick. Are you ready for me?"

"Mm-hmm," I say as I try once again to back my ass toward him. This earns me another slap on the ass. Before

I can protest, he slams into me, and I nearly topple over onto the bed. He easily catches me as he slides in and out of me at a leisurely pace. He gives me a few slow strokes before slamming into me again. I love how he switches up his fucking—keeping my pussy on edge. "God, yes!" I shout. It's nice not to have to be quiet. There is nobody to mistakenly hear us.

Phoenix wraps my hair in his fist and yanks my head back as he begins to drive into me deeper. I can't help but slam back against him. This feels fucking amazing. Just as my legs begin to quiver, he stops and once again stills my hips. He leans forward and massages my breast, but that is not what I want. He returns to his steady strokes, but I need him to pound me. I need him to fuck me mercilessly. He has awakened the woman in me that I never knew existed.

JUST WHEN I THINK I CAN NO LONGER TAKE HIS deliberate teasing, he slaps my ass once more. I'm beginning to see this is his thing. His hips piston as he delivers the most punishing strokes imaginable. He grabs my hips and digs deep. I relax into his assault on my pussy, and the feeling is so freaking euphoric. Stars dance behind my eyes, and my head becomes hazy as I reach the pinnacle of an abyss that I've yet to feel until now.

"Fuck, yes. That's it, baby," Phoenix coaxes. I'm speechless. I'm nearly limp when I feel him find his own release. I can feel his cock throbbing in me. It seems to go on forever. He finally pulls out, and we both fall to the bed. He pulls me to him. "Oh, don't think I'm done with you. I'm just getting started. Tonight I will introduce you to my stamina, and you will love it."

"Oh, really?" I ask when I'm able to find my voice. "Why is that?"

"Just the obvious reasons. Multiple orgasms." He chuckles.

"Hmm. Who says I need multiple orgasms, and does this stamina have a name?" I tease.

"Uh, you don't need to say anything. Your pussy begs for my dick all on its own." I can hear the smirk in his voice. "And my stamina doesn't need a name. When it's that amazing, it just is...no formalities needed." I can't help but laugh at his cockiness. I know he is giving me shit right now, but I have a feeling I'm about to get real acquainted with his stamina.

CHAPTER FOURTEEN
Phoenix

The early morning light filters through the bedroom window, and with it comes ambiguous regret. I don't regret bringing Harlow to at least five orgasms before she passed out from exhaustion. No, that is a memory I will hold on for some time to come. I was even tempted to show her a glimpse of my dark side—my kink for control. In the end, I decided against it. I don't think she would have been ready for that. That being said, I broke two of my fucking rules. I don't do sleepovers, and I sure as hell don't cuddle. Last night I did both. This woman is changing me, and I don't like it. In reality, she means more than just some groupie, but my rules are set for a reason. I can't break any more of them—not for her—not for anyone. We've already fucked twice. I'm not sure if I can allow the third opportunity that I normally give before a woman is cut off. Harlow has managed to slip past my terms once, and I have to regain control. I don't want to hurt her, so I need to end this before it's too late. She is beautiful, and sex with her is unquantifiable, but I have to stop my involvement with her. Having her come by the lake house will surely be awkward for a while.

"Morning," Harlow says groggily as she wipes the sleep from her eyes. "What time is it?"

"Morning. It's just after seven," I say simply. I hop out of bed and find my clothes that are lying around on the floor.

"Where's the fire, stallion?" she jokes as I quickly get dressed.

"I need to get you back to school. I have something to do this morning." I pull my shirt over my head, but I don't miss the disappointment in her eyes. It solidifies my earlier thought. To continue things with her would make "that look" much worse later. I'm an asshole, and she needs someone good. There is no happily ever after with me—only fucking, and her time is up. "I'll check us out of the hotel and meet you downstairs, out front."

"Sure." Her tone is dry. She gets up and puts her clothes on just as fast; only she isn't looking at me now. I think she senses the change the day has brought about. I want to reassure her, but I can't. I leave her to finish getting dressed, and I feel like shit.

When I walk through the door, the guys are ready to give me a hard time. They know about my rules.

"So who is the lucky woman who made you break your 'fuck-n-go'?" Killian jokes.

"Yeah, must have been some piece of ass," Asher chimes in. If he only knew and with who, that grin would be wiped off his face right now. Ren eyes me suspiciously. I blew off the kiss he saw between Harlow and me as temporary insanity. My excuse was that I was horny, and she was there. I told him that I had come to my senses, and nothing happened.

I can see the wheels churning in his head as he suspects now that may have been a lie.

"It's not what you think, fuckers. I do have other friends, you know? I got a little shitfaced with my buddy Sevyn while we played *Destiny* on the Xbox, and I ended up sleeping it off." I shake my head at their nosiness of my sex life. "No pussy is worth breaking my rules for," I reassure. That lie rolls off my tongue like it has been rehearsed. I've told myself this so many times, yet this morning it wasn't the case. I'm trying not to let it get to me, so I'm not going to give these guys any indication that I was with a woman. I'd never heard the end of it.

"Who is this Sevyn person? I'm beginning to think he is a figment of your imagination," Ren chides.

"Whatever, asshole." I flip him off and make my way

to the kitchen. I was supposed to have eaten already, so even the timing of my meals is off. *Fuck.*

"Well, why haven't we met this dude? Why are you hiding him like a lover?" Killian joins in.

"Shut the fuck up. He has no interest in hanging with you douche bags. And you have seen him."

I ignore their questions of when, because the truth is, they have seen him—more than once. They will never formally meet him, and I can't share our real connection or what we're involved in. I'm actually meeting him at noon.

HE IS A SEPARATE PART OF MY LIFE THEY CAN NEVER BE privy to. The only reason they even know he exists is because they kept questioning where I would disappear to sometimes. It's not their business—they're not my keepers, but I don't want them to think the worst. When possible drug addiction ideas started to circulate, I knew I had to give them a bone. Hell, they wanted to stage an intervention. We have a strict no drugs policy. No exceptions. We don't want to be your typical rock band and allow drugs to fuck off our opportunities before we even start. I didn't feel like making up a name—too hard to keep up with, so I told them I had a friend named Sevyn. I told them I was helping him with something and to let it drop. For the most part, they respect my wishes not to talk about him. This morning, they just feel like giving me shit.

"Come on, Killian. Your ass is going with me to buy groceries. Let Phoenix and his mystery man have their privacy," he jokes. Asher pats me on the shoulder and shakes his head.

"Ignore those two." He grabs his water bottle off the table. "Hold on, dipshits, I'm going with you. You guys need chaperoning for the shit you like to buy." Asher isn't kidding. These guys stock up on more snacks than real food. At least with him going, I know he'll get what I need for my meal preps. Once the guys are out the door, I eat, pack a few meals, and get ready to meet Sevyn.

~

Harlow

I'M SITTING ON MY BED, TRYING TO FIGURE OUT WHAT went wrong with Phoenix. Things have changed in an instant. Was this all a game? I finally let down my guard and throw caution to the wind and had sex with him—twice. Now it is as if he is done with me. He couldn't get out of that hotel room with me fast enough. He could barely even look at me, and the ride back to the dorm was quiet and strained. Was I not good enough for him? I don't know what to think.

"So, how was it?" Irelyn says, jumping on my bed. She wasn't here when I got back, so I thought I had time to think.

"What?" I grab my folder off the dresser and pretend

to look through my syllabus to see what upcoming assignments I have. I can't look at her right now. I'm afraid she will see the insecurities that have taken residence in my mind.

"Cut the shit. You guys fucked again. You left early yesterday and didn't come back until this morning." She yanks the folder from me. "Come on. I'm your best friend. Tell me what's going on. You're not catching feelings for this guy, are you?" I don't know what I'm feeling. Of course I didn't think this thing between us could mature into anything. It was just fucking, and now it's over. He's a manwhore. I gave in to what my body wanted and let myself have a piece of his sexy ass.

"There are definitely no feelings involved, Irelyn. It was just sex. I was horny, and he wanted to fuck. I needed to brush off the old cobwebs." I try to joke, but my laugh falls flat.

"Are you sure?" She eyes me suspiciously—unsure of what to believe. "Because you do know that his type will never change. The more famous he gets, the more pussy he will get thrown at him."

"Yes, Irelyn. I know this. I'm not a fool." I tell her about our first hookup and then everything about yesterday. I leave out the part about his mood change this morning. I just tell her we ended it, but I don't explain how or why because I'm not sure of that myself.

"Well, good. I'm glad you're back on the proverbial sex

horse, so to speak." She has no idea how off the horse I've been. She goes off on a tangent about me getting back on the dating scene, but then my phone rings.

"Hello?" I wave my hand to silence her because it's Asher.

"Hey, sis. What are you up to?" I can hear the guys in the background. I wonder if Phoenix is with them.

"Nothing. Just talking with Irelyn. What's up?"

"Well, I'm out grocery shopping with the guys, and we've decided to fire up the grill while the weather is still nice. I was wondering if you and Irelyn would like to come hang out for the day. I can come and get you and bring you back later tonight."

"Uh, I don't know, Asher." I'm not ready to see Phoenix again. It'll be a hard pill to swallow if he behaves like he did this morning.

"Aw, come on. I don't want to interrupt your plans, but we may have a reason to celebrate. I wasn't going to say anything yet, but I want you here." He lets out a sigh. "If you can't, I understand."

"No. We don't have any plans for today, so we can come." I give Irelyn a pleading look. She has to go with me.

"Great. We're checking out now, so I'll be there in an hour." I can hear him telling the guys that he is going to be picking us up.

"See you then." We say our goodbyes and hang up.

"WHAT DID YOU JUST VOLUNTEER ME FOR?" IRELYN smirks.

"The guys are grilling and apparently have some news to share. I can't go by myself. You have to go." I don't have to explain the awkwardness I would feel with Phoenix. Even without knowing the entire story, she gets it. If I'm lucky, maybe he won't even be there. He did say he had something he had to do. "Asher will be here in an hour."

"Fine. I was planning on soaking up some warm rays and hottie watching on the campus lawn, so you owe me," she kids.

"Well, tomorrow we'll grab a blanket and hottie watch together," I promise, and she grins from ear to ear. An old oak tree by the library is a popular spot for students to hang out under while they study. Irelyn likes to take her blanket and just people watch—hot guys, to be specific.

SHE HAS BEEN TRYING TO GET ME TO PARTAKE IN THIS useless activity, but I always turn her down. I know I could have gotten her to go with me without that asinine promise, but I thought it was only fair that I return the favor. I decide to go with a simple tank top and jeans. I French braid my hair and call it a day. Irelyn opts for a tube dress and wedge sandals. I sometimes envy her chic style, but I'd rather be comfortable. After we're dressed and ready to go, we head downstairs to wait for Asher.

~

So far, so good, no sign of Phoenix. Asher is out on the deck with Ren, starting up the grill while Killian seasons the meat and veggies. Irelyn makes herself at home on the white leather sofa. She flips through the channels on the television, trying to find something interesting. I grab a glass and pour myself some wine before joining her. It's a little past noon, but it's not too early to start drinking. I have a feeling I'm going to need it. My premonition is correct. I haven't even finished my glass when Phoenix walks in with some leggy brunette. Her heels click on the tile when she walks. Her fitted dress leaves nothing to wonder about. She is definitely stacked, but where the hell is she coming from looking like that? Even Irelyn is shocked. We exchange glances, and I know she is wondering the same thing that I am.

Who is this woman to Phoenix? The better question is—is she what he had to do this morning? She flicks her hair to one side as she waits to be introduced. Phoenix is beaming as he steps forward. Asher and Ren reenter the house, just in time for Phoenix's introduction.

"Everyone, this is Desiree Roberson." The guys give her a welcoming hello while Irelyn and I half raise our hands in a wave. "Desiree is with Pretty Boy Rock and has heard good things about our band."

"Heck yeah!" the fellas chant heartily. Pretty Boy Rock is a pretty big deal. They're among the best record labels in the industry for producing rock music.

"Desiree got in contact with me and wanted to meet up today to talk about our music. She's heard a few of our cover songs and is interested in hearing more of our original music," Phoenix adds. I'm happy for them. This could be their big break. I watch as Desiree rubs the top of his shoulder, and he looks over and smiles at her. The scene before me doesn't sit right. My stomach churns at the thought he may have been with her more than to discuss a possible record deal earlier. Maybe he used his assets to sway the decision more in their favor. She looks mighty comfortable with him.

"We have some of our stuff recorded," Asher offers. "We also have our own makeshift studio if you want to hear us live," he offers excitedly.

"Oh, no. I'm not staying long. I just wanted to meet you guys. I'm coming Friday to see you guys play at Club Luxe," she assures. The guys introduce themselves, one by one, and tell about their position in the band. I can hear the enthusiasm in their voices. I can only imagine how ecstatic they must feel to be recognized by such a big label. Asher briefly introduces Irelyn and me and then tries again to get her to stay, but she declines.

"I'll leave you gentlemen to your afternoon. Nice meeting you ladies, as well," she says as an afterthought. Irelyn and I feign fake smiles and wave goodbye. I watch as her hips sway again as she walks out the door. The guys all walk her out. *Yes. It took all of them.*

Irelyn looks at me when they're all out of sight. "Did you get a load of her?" She shakes her head like she's trying to clear it.

"Something is definitely off with her. She seems like the nicety type. Nice-nasty. Hidden agenda. I don't know, but she makes my hackles go up." I can't put a finger on the negative vibes she inspires. They're just there.

"Not to mention, she had her claws in Phoenix. She's probably already fucked him. Maybe even how the meeting came about," she ponders. My face falls before I can school my expression. "Shit, that was insensitive, Harlow. But see, this is why it is best you cut all ties. If they get this record deal, things are going to change for them real quick." I know she is telling the truth, so why does it feel like I'm being stabbed in the chest? I'm not supposed to care.

CHAPTER FIFTEEN
Phoenix

The look on Harlow's face as I introduced Desiree to the band was telling. She was jealous. I didn't expect her to be there. Asher must have invited her over. When Desiree put her hand on my shoulder, I saw the slightest of flinches from Harlow; one that could have been missed if you weren't watching closely. I bet anything she thinks I slept with this woman, so that leads me to another conclusion. What a mess? I have to keep my distance from her today. I don't have answers for her or have any idea how to move forward right now. Yup. Avoidance is key until I can get the hell out of here.

When we get back upstairs, I don't even look at her. I know hurt no matter how much it's masked, and I know exactly why it's there. "Killian, grab a beer and come down to the lake with me, fucker."

"Sure. We can discuss how you really came to meet

Miss Desiree," he taunts. "Seriously, though, we need a game plan for this weekend. Maybe even squeeze in writing a new song to showcase, if we can."

"Already on it, man. I want us to have at least a few of our original songs ready and only our best covers."

"Agreed," Asher joins in. Killian grabs a beer and heads toward the lake with me. We leave Asher and Ren with the girls.

"So how did you come in contact with Desiree?" he asks when we're finally alone.

"Mutual friend," I answer simply as I take a swig of my beer.

Yup, I'm fucking off my diet regimen, but today calls for a celebration. It was fucked today from the start when I didn't have my ass at home to start my first meal on time.

"Sevyn?" His face lights up like he just had an epiphany or some shit. "You said you were meeting him today, and you came back with her. He's the mutual friend, isn't he?" It's weird hearing the name, especially since he has no idea how close he is.

"Yes. Sevyn has done business with her in another capacity and told her all about us. She was intrigued, to say the least."

"That guy is alright with me. We may give you shit for not bringing him around, but that was good looking out. I hope she signs us."

"She is one of the managers who introduces the talent and manages them, but she is not the one who actually does the signing," I explain.

"Yeah, but if she is interested, she can get us in front of the right people. We will take it from there. I have all the confidence in our talent, so same difference." I agree with Killian. The band's sound is pretty impressive, and we don't look like your typical rockers, for the most part, except Ren. His appearance screams rocker with his black Mohawk and piercings. Too bad, he really is a big softie. I have a song in mind that has been playing on a loop in my mind.

I CAN PROBABLY HAVE IT FINISHED BY TONIGHT, SO I hope it's well-received. "Yeah. I think we have this one in the bag. We just need to get in front of those executives. We'll have them eating out of our hand," I say.

"Especially if they're more of the female persuasion than men. You can use your magical charms." Killian nearly chokes on his beer from laughing so hard.

"Whatever, fucker. We don't need charm when we got the talent."

"Your pretty face will help," he teases. "You know the women always see you first. Our asses get the leftovers." He wants to give me shit, so I dish it right back.

"It's not the face, bro. It's this dick. I think the word has gotten around about my anaconda, and now they all want a piece. Hard to keep that shit a secret." He laughs even harder, and I join him.

"Okay, let's change the subject, dude. We are not going to discuss your dick and how big you think it is."

"Oh, I don't have to think. I have to fit this motherfucker in my jeans every day." He gives me a look of disgust, and I wink at him before slamming back the rest of my beer. The group joins us, so we indeed change the subject.

Harlow sits across from me with a glass of wine in hand. The discussion quickly turns to football and our opposing love for the Cowboys and the Eagles.

SURPRISINGLY, IRELYN IS A DALLAS COWBOYS FAN, LIKE Ren and me, so it makes it three against two. Asher and Killian are traitors. The game starts in a few hours, and we're all making bets on which team we think will win. Dallas is on a losing streak right now, but they're my team, no matter what. Harlow looks on, but she doesn't join the conversation. She just sips on her wine and listens to our craziness.

"So who do root for, Harlow?" Killian asks in attempt to include her in our conversation.

"I don't," she says simply. "I don't know much about the game." She looks at me briefly but quickly looks away.

"Tragic," he retorts. "We have to teach you about football, girl. Irelyn, you're slacking, woman."

"It's not her thing." She grins at her friend. "And that's

okay, so hush." After a beat of silence, everyone goes back to making their wagers. Not for money, but for bragging rights. I get up to go get another beer.

"You guys want anything while I'm up?" I ask. They all shake their head, so I make my way back to the house. I scarf down a sandwich while I'm in here. I'm about to grab the beer I came in for when I turn and see Harlow. She is standing there looking unsure, but clearly with something to say.

"Are you going to tell me what this morning was all about?" she asks.

"What do you mean?"

"Why were you in a hurry to get away from me?" I don't know what to tell her. This is more than just a little awkward.

"I can't do this with you right now," I say, trying to push past her, but she stops me.

"Just say it," she says, getting flustered.

"What do you want me to say, huh?"

"That you fucked me, and now you're done with me. Just have the balls to say it's over, instead of running away like a fucking coward. It was just sex, for fuck's sake. Just do me the decency of ending it." I see the unshed tears glistening in her eyes, and I'm about to lose my shit. I don't get off on hurting a woman. I hate that I'm in this fucking position.

"Yeah. Okay. It's over. There. Now are you happy? I've said it. You will find somebody better than—"

"Save me the 'I'll find somebody better' bullshit," she cuts me off. "I never thought of us as more than a fuck anyway. I just wanted to hear the words. Don't brush me off like one of your goddamn groupies." She raises her voice slightly, and although she claims that she has gotten what she wanted, clearly things are not as settled in her mind as she tries to pretend it is.

"I have to go. I can't do this. Tell the guys I left." I can hear her hollering behind my back.

"Yeah. Do what you do best—run." I don't acknowledge her last statement. I leave her alone with her anger, and hope to God the guys didn't hear her.

~

Harlow

I STAND HERE, NOT KNOWING WHAT THE FUCK TO FEEL. I can't believe I confronted Phoenix. I didn't plan on it, but the liquid courage of my wine demanded answers. His nonchalant, what did I do attitude pissed me off. Oh, and that "I will find someone" crap made me want to strangle him. How dare he treat me like one of his groupies that he is done with and has to let down easy? Let's call it what it was. It was a fuck—nothing more and nothing less. So why the hell am I so bothered by his dismissal? I knew the score before I opened my legs. I can't go back outside and listen to them talk about football. I pull out my phone and call Irelyn.

"Hey."

"Where are you?" I can hear the guys still talking about football in the background.

"In the kitchen. I'm calling because I'm ready to go. Tell Asher, please. I'm sorry to cut our time short, but I'll explain later."

"It's okay. I have to get back to studying for a test tomorrow, too," she says loudly. I'm guessing this is for the guy's benefit, so they don't question our sudden need to go home. "We need to get back, Asher," I hear Irelyn say. She makes up a story about me getting a call from some members of our study group looking for us and that we have a test tomorrow. I'm glad I'm not the one who had to tell him that lie. I don't think I could have kept a straight face.

∼

"Okay, spill," Irelyn prompts once we are behind the closed doors of our room. "First Phoenix leaves, and then all of a sudden you need to leave, too. What gives?" I don't know how to approach the subject since I withheld some parts of my morning with Phoenix. I guess I just get it over with and tell her everything. I always do, for the most part.

"So maybe I didn't tell you everything this morning," I begin.

"I knew it. I can always tell, but I don't push. What did that asshat do?"

"Well, everything else I said was true. The sex was amazing. I mean, the orgasms were mind-blowing, and there were too many to count. The only thing is, this morning, he was a different person. He wasn't the attentive lover who put my pleasure before his own. He didn't look at me like I was something special. Instead, he looked perturbed. He was anxious to get away from me. He couldn't get his clothes on fast enough. It felt as though he regretted last night." I plop on my bed. I can feel the anger within me start to surface again.

"Oh, babe. I'm so sorry." She comes and sits next to me on the bed.

"I didn't plan on saying anything to him. It was just a fuck. But then the more wine I drank, the more I wanted answers. I wanted him to just fucking tell me it was over, so I cornered him in the kitchen." I chuckle sadly.

"Shit. What did he say?" Irelyn's eyebrows are nearly in her hairline.

"He looked taken off guard, at first—like he didn't realize he'd done anything wrong. Then the cockiness appeared after I dealt with the brush-off. My thing is... don't treat me like a fucking groupie. We had sex, it's done, say so, and we both move on. Don't treat me like something you regret."

"Forget him. He probably just sucks at the 'after sex' part. His loss." She grabs my hand and squeezes. "You know it isn't you, so don't give it a second thought. You had a chance to fuck that sexy beast, and now you can move on. You knew he wasn't the type to settle with. Think of it as whetting your appetite before getting the main dish. We will find you someone more suitable." There's that phrase again of "finding someone." I don't want to fucking find someone. This isn't a free-for-all. I felt something with Phoenix, so I let myself have him. I don't want to fuck with guys for the hell of it or for the sake of being in a relationship. I don't regret anything. It was fun while it lasted, so why am I still bummed? Why can't I pull myself out of this funk? Surely, I haven't caught feelings. *Ugh, I don't know what the fuck I'm feeling.* I'm just going to have to stay away from the lake house until the feeling passes. I really do hope Pretty Boy Rock signs them. That would be an amazing opportunity for them.

MY INNER THOUGHTS ARE INTERRUPTED BY IRELYN trying to convince me to go to a house party next weekend. Ordinarily, I would say no. Feeling down, I decide to do something out of the norm.

"Sure, I'll go."

"What?" she asks, stunned. "I was prepared to beg,

and you go and surprise me with being all easy. First, you agree to hottie watch with me and now go to a house party. What have you done with my best friend?" She giggles.

"A little change is good. Not saying it will be permanent, but I'm willing to try to have a little fun this semester."

"Okay. We have to go shopping on Thursday. All you ever wear are those jeans. We need to accentuate your assets." She gives me a huge smile and bats her eyes. She is really pushing her luck, but I let her make it. If she wants to go shopping and make me look like slutty Barbie with her for the night, I'll indulge. I have to admit that my mentality has come a long way.

"Fine." I watch as she clasps her hand over her mouth. She gets up off the bed and does a celebratory dance. Then she stops mid-move and turns to look at me.

"Oh, one more thing." She approaches me cautiously. "While you were in the kitchen with Phoenix, Asher mentioned picking us up on Friday so that we can watch their performance. Apparently, they're going to be doing more of their original songs for Desiree, and he wants us there for luck."

THE SMILE ON MY FACE DROPS. "IRELYN, I CAN'T." ALL I can imagine is seeing Phoenix flirt with countless women and getting up to his usual after the show.

"Harlow. Asher said 'us,' but he really wants you there

for support. This can be the night that changes their lives, and he wants his sister there to witness it. You can't let the fuck you had with Phoenix twice make you turn your back on your brother. That would crush him. What excuse could you possibly give—what could be more important?" Of course she is right. I can't do that to Asher, even if I could think of a valid excuse. *Shit.*

"You're right." I hang my head in defeat. This thing with Phoenix is bothering me way more than it should.

"Hey. Hey. None of that. You pick your head up. We're going shopping Thursday. I will make sure you are a knockout for Friday night. Phoenix won't know what hit him. He will regret that he was such a douche, and he lost his chance to hit that," she says, pointing toward my vagina. Okay, that makes me smile. Yes, his loss. I just thought of a plan.

"I think I'll just be the biggest flirt on Friday night. Show him, he is not the only dick out there. I'll show him that I can be sexy like those skanks he attracts, and how he lost his chance with me." Suddenly, I'm in a better mood. Why should I let one man determine my worth? Make me feel inferior? I can't wait until Friday to put my plan into action.

CHAPTER SIXTEEN

Harlow

We're sitting in the Escalade, and my nerves are taking over. Asher's eyes almost fell out of his head when he saw me, but he didn't say much. I know that he is treading lightly, not wanting to bruise my self-esteem. He couldn't fake his reaction, though. I could see the curiosity in his eyes. I'm wearing a red strapless bandage dress that has my tits busting over the top and just barely covers my ass. I know I'm going to be pulling it down all night, but not so much where the girls spill out. The black pumps and clutch purse complete the look. Irelyn did my makeup and hair. I must admit I look hot. I didn't know I could look this way.

"You look gorgeous," she says, reading my thoughts. "But nobody is going to see that if you stay in this truck."

"I think you need a coat," Asher mumbles under his breath.

"Oh, hush. She looks hot." Irelyn blows him a kiss, and he gets out of the truck.

"Ugh," he grunts. I'm pretty sure he doesn't want to hear about his sister being hot. I finally get out of the truck because I know I can't hide here forever. Irelyn gets out and joins me. Her black dress is similar to mine but with straps. Also because her ass isn't as big, her dress has a little more length.

"Come on, sex kitten. Let's go knock 'em dead." Ugh. I feel like Asher now. I'm already starting to regret this decision. I need some liquid courage and quick.

We go into the bar, but the guys haven't taken the stage yet. They usually go on about ten, and it's just after nine. "Let's get a drink," Irelyn suggests.

"That is an excellent idea. You read my mind." I'm proud of my conquest of these heels. You'd think I wear them all the time. I sashay my ass like I saw Desiree do this past weekend, and Irelyn laughs.

"Let me guess who that is supposed to be."

"Desiree," we say in unison.

"You have too much ass for that walk, babe. You'd give every guy within a mile radius a raging hard-on."

"If a guy was a mile away, he couldn't see my ass, you moron. What are you trying to say?" I gently push her, and she is in hysterics.

"That was a compliment," she gasps between chuckles.

"Let's just get our drink, cray-cray." We make it to the bar, and I'm happy to park my ass in the seat. I said I could walk in these heels. I never said anything about them being comfortable. These are definitely "get-your-ass-somewhere-and-sit-down" shoes. The bar girl is the same one from last time, so she doesn't card us, although Irelyn made her twenty-one this summer. I order a mojito, and Irelyn orders a cosmo. We are two drinks in and on our third before the guys take the stage. They open with Memphis May Fire's, *Speechless*. The women are already rushing the stage.

PHOENIX IS WEARING HIS SIGNATURE LOOK. HIS FITTED white T-shirt hugs his chest and abs, showcasing every muscle. I can see the bulging of his biceps as he grips the mic. Because I'm sitting back here, I can ogle him without being obvious. His jeans sit low, and his muscular thighs are drool-worthy. His fucking body is just amazing. No matter how much of a douche he may be, he is sexy as fuck. I can't help but continue my perusal. His hair is tapered short on the sides with a little length spiked on top. His goatee is trimmed neatly. Adding to all this, I know firsthand that he can fuck, so he has the full package. Well, almost, he's still a manwhore.

"*It's a mystery, too good to be true. I find my purpose when I look at you,*" Phoenix begins. The rasp in his voice demands attention. It's as sexy as he is.

"Enjoying the view?" Irelyn asks, interrupting my lustful thoughts.

"Whatever," I reply nonchalantly

"Oh, I don't blame you. He is hot as hell, but so are you. Come on. Let's move closer." She doesn't give me a chance to protest. She is off her barstool in seconds. We take our drinks and walk to the back of the room where the stage is. I watch as Phoenix rubs his abs and uses eye contact to flirt with the women. Irelyn obscurely pokes me in the side and uses her head to gesture for me to look to her right.

I SEE DESIREE PERCHED AT ONE OF THE FEW TABLES OFF to the side of the stage with her legs crossed. She has two guys in suits sitting next to her. I can see her smiling as she takes in the band's performance. That has to be a good sign, right? I sure hope so. Regardless of my dismissal by Phoenix, I want the guys to succeed. If Desiree's expression is anything to go by, they are knocking it out of the park. They sing a couple more cover songs before they mix in some of their original stuff. These guys are amazingly talented. I stay hidden within the crowd until familiar lyrics fill the air.

I KEEP TELLING MYSELF IT'S THE LAST TIME
Each time it proves to be a lie
The darkness pulls me deeper into the shadows

It won't let me see the light.
It's a never-ending battle that I can't seem to win,
Maybe one day I'll defeat the devil...
The monster that lives within.

I WANT TO LEAVE IT ALL BEHIND
　I want to leave it all behind
　I want to leave it all behind

TAKE BACK CONTROL... MAKE MY ESCAPE FROM THESE demons I face.
　This is my warning to you.
　This is your chance to be free.
　Don't give in to the hunger I crave
　because I can't be sated.

I WANT TO LEAVE IT ALL BEHIND
　I want to leave it all behind
　I want to leave it all behind

YOU'RE MY WEAKNESS. THIS IS CLEAR TO SEE
　I try to hide the demons from you that live inside me
　You're getting too close to finding out my secret
　And now I have to let you go, so that you may never know
　　　　　　　　　　　. . .

Take back control... Make my escape from these demons I face.
> *This is my warning to you.*
> *This is your chance to be free.*
> *Don't give in to the hunger I crave*
> *because I can't be sated.*

I want to leave it all behind
> *I want to leave it all behind*
> *I want to leave it all behind*

Before I know it, I'm closer to the stage than I thought. Not the front row, because it is a frenzy up there, but close enough for him to see me. I see the moment he does a double take. I forgot all about this sexy persona I've taken on for the night. These are the lyrics he shared with me that nobody else had heard that day at the arboretum. The lyrics are finished and are beautifully arranged with the band. His voice is tender and vulnerable right *now*. I can't stop the tears from welling in my eyes. Crap. I can't mess up my makeup. Luckily, I'm able to keep the tears from falling.

Phoenix holds my stare as he pours his heart out into the chorus. An unfamiliar feeling passes through me and squeezes my heart. Suddenly, this is all too much. Memories from that day flood my mind, as well as the other few times he showed me a different man than he shows everyone else.

I back away from the stage slowly until I back into Irelyn. "This song is amazing. It's so different from their other stuff."

"Yeah," I agree dryly.

"It is perfect for Desiree to see. It shows their versatility. These guys can rock hard, but also be vulnerable and sultry. I think it's hot. Not to mention, I'm seeing Killian in a new light. The way his fingers are strumming that guitar is making my lady parts tingle."

"Ugh, Irelyn. TMI." So it seems my friend has set her sights on Killian. He's sweet enough but is equally a manwhore like Phoenix.

The guys switch it up to Until the Ribbon Break's version of "One Way or Another," and it's sexy as fuck as Phoenix's voice lowers an octave briefly. They're really showing their range tonight. Unfortunately, with it, his flirtatiousness makes a reappearance. He kneels at the front of the stage, and the women break their necks to touch him. He's really keeping security on their toes tonight as the women have to repeatedly be told to back up. God, I can only imagine once he really gets famous. It's bad enough he already has a fan club. Those women at the front of the stage are the same ones from the last time I was here, and the time before that, with a few new additions. The thirstiness among them is contagious, it seems.

I watch as he leans forward and uses one finger to stroke between the cleavage one blonde has squeezed together with her hands.

She squeals at the contact. The women next to her try to offer up their tits as well, but he just winks at them as he backs away from the edge of the stage. The special moment I thought I shared with him in a room full of people has been officially ruined.

"Look at those thirsty bitches," Irelyn says in disgust.

"You're in my head again, woman. I was just thinking that." I shake my head. "Come on, I want another drink." I don't wait for her to answer. I make a beeline for the bar, and she follows me. I see a couple of college frat guys I recognize from campus. I don't know their names, but I've seen them around before.

"James, Mike? What are you AKL boys doing here?" Of course Irelyn would know who they are. She is such a social butterfly.

"Alpha Kappa Lambda in the house," the blond hoots.

"Don't mind Mike," the ginger says. "Who's your friend?" So the redhead must be James. Irelyn looks over at me and smiles.

"This is my best friend, Harlow," she says a little too excitedly. I see her matchmaker wheels turning. I admit James is cute—red hair, blue eyes, and freckles. He has a nice build too. Not as nice as Phoenix's, but muscular enough. I'm not really looking to meet or date anyone, but he could be just what I need to give Phoenix a taste of his own medicine. I can do a little flirting of my own.

"Hello, Harlow. Such a pretty name. Nice to meet you." He and Mike exchange glances. Yeah, this one is just as slick. He may or may not have his own fan club of women, but I can tell he is a whore magnet all the same. The conversation seems normal enough, but it drips with undertones of mischief. His eyes roam my body, but I can't even blame him. My shit is on display for him to ogle.

"Same here," I say, trying to sound interested as I shake his hand. Mike introduces himself, and we all have a seat at the bar. I'm glad because these heels aren't made for much standing around either.

"So what are you ladies drinking?" James asks.

"Mojito," I reply. I try to stay with the same drink and not mix.

"Long Island," Irelyn says. Of course, she has no problem switching it up. I have yet to see mixing alcohol be a problem for her, though. The guys order our drinks, and I look over at the stage where the band is now performing The Color Morale's "The Dying Hymn." Phoenix's vocal range really is ridiculous. Those guys can go from soft rock to hard-core without any effort. They keep the crowd guessing and have a little something for everyone to rock to.

In a matter of seconds, Phoenix is looking right at me. I cross my legs and lean closer to James until he takes a seat next to me to wait for our drinks. Let the flirting begin.

I CONTROL THE URGE TO FLINCH AT THE FEEL OF JAMES'S hand pressed against my lower back. He's all smiles as he tells me about his fraternity. He thinks I'm impressed, and I don't tell him any different. I giggle at the appropriate times and rest a hand on his knee. I don't know if Phoenix can see this spectacle I'm putting on from the stage, but I hope it's not in vain. Irelyn winks at me, but I hope she knows this act is for show. I'm not interested in James.

"So what do you like to do?" James asks.

"Read." I take a sip of my drink and bat my eyelashes. This is really hard work. How can women do this all the time? It's exhausting.

"That's it?" he quizzes.

"Mm-hmm."

"You're such the talker," he muses. "What do you like to read?"

"Romance novels. Erotica, to be exact," I lie. I mainly read paranormal to escape reality, but whatever gets him going. I might as well have fun.

"Oh, the dirty books. It's always the quiet ones. I bet

you get some fantastic ideas from them." He wags his eyebrows. "Any fantasies you want to fulfill?" What a creep...such a gentleman this one.

"No. I'm good." I'm not going to even lead him on. Whatever conclusion he draws about how tonight is going will be derived on his own. "So, do you play any sports?" I recognize his football class ring and take the chance that he still plays.

This changes the subject, and he is all too happy to talk more about himself and football. After a couple more drinks, I can feel the buzz of the alcohol. Okay, maybe a little more than just a little buzz. I'm not fall-on-my-ass drunk, but I'm definitely heading in that direction. It's been a while since I've allowed myself to drink this much. I blame James and his incessant talking. The band's music has long faded, and music from the overhead speakers has taken its place. I know their set is over, but I'm not sure what time it is. I don't even want to think about the after-show ass Phoenix is probably getting right now.

"You ladies want to get out of here?" Mike asks over Irelyn's shoulder.

"And go where?" Yeah, I'm living on the edge right now. I don't plan on doing anything with James, but I wouldn't mind making Phoenix wonder why we aren't riding home with them. It's not like these guys are ax murderers. They go to our school.

"I thought maybe we could grab a bite to eat and then find an after-hours pool hall," Mike suggests.

"Good idea," James says in agreement.

"I'm down," I say, getting off my barstool. The fucking floor sways underneath my feet.

"Are you sure, Harlow?" Irelyn asks hesitantly. "You look kind of hammered."

"Absolutely. And I'm fine. Yes, I have a buzz, but I'm completely with it."

"Okay, if you're sure then—" She doesn't get a chance to finish that statement. Her eyes go wide, and I feel him before I see him. Phoenix's hands snake around my waist and pull me to him.

CHAPTER SEVENTEEN

Harlow

"Where do you think you're going?" he whispers. His breath against my ear ignites my traitorous body.

"With these guys," I say, pointing at James and Mike.

"Wrong answer, sweetheart." Phoenix pulls me back into him even further, and this time the thin barrier of my dress between us doesn't miss the impressive bulge in his jeans. "Sorry to break up your plans, fellas, but these ladies came with us and will be leaving with us."

"It's the ladies' choice," James replies, puffing up his chest. Phoenix steps around me and squares off with him. With one look, you can tell it wouldn't even be an effort. This guy has to be crazy because Phoenix would pummel his ass. The size of Phoenix's biceps alone should be a clue.

"I don't think so. Her brother is out back and asked me to let them know we're leaving. There doesn't have to be a problem unless you make it one." James is about to smart off, but Irelyn steps between them.

"Uh, it's okay. Another time, guys. It's late, and he's right. We came with them," Irelyn says to defuse the situation.

"Harlow, a word please!" Phoenix pulls me toward the opposite of where the guys are waiting. "Irelyn, we'll catch up with you in a sec," he says, looking over his shoulder. I double my steps, trying to match his stride. I only agree to go with him to get him away from the dumbass that was foolish enough to think he could challenge him.

"Where are we going?" I'm too buzzed for this shit. It's becoming blatantly obvious that these heels and alcohol don't mix as I work to remain upright.

PHOENIX DOESN'T SAY A WORD. HIS JAW CLENCHES, AND for the first time, I recognize that he is upset with me. We turn into a hallway to the left. He opens the door to a dark room and pushes me in. *What the fuck?* Some light from the street shines through from the above windows to clue me in that we're in a storage room.

"What the fuck are you wearing, Harlow?" Phoenix is on me again in seconds.

"I...I..." I stutter. I don't know what to say. His voice is different—strangled. His demeanor is different too, more aggressive.

"Did you wear this for me?" His hand inches my dress up until my thong-clad ass is on display. He turns me, facing away from him, and pushes me against the shelf. "Answer me, Harlow. You've gotten my attention. You've had it all night. I had to give the performance of my life with my dick hard." He rubs his dick against me, and even through the jeans, it's a turn-on. This is not supposed to be happening, yet I'm powerless to stop it.

He slips a hand in the front of my panties and begins to rub my clit. My hips follow his ministrations.

"Yes." I admit that the dress was for him. Only he has managed to awaken a woman in me that I don't recognize—pull me out of the shell I thought I was destined to reside in.

"Yes, Sir." He corrects. *What. The. Fuck?*

"Sir?" I question.

"Hmm. Now you're catching on."

"What are you talking about, Phoenix?" He rubs harder against my clit, and I moan.

"You wanted him, and so you shall get him," he says cryptically. He continues to work my clit until my juices are flowing. I know I should be putting a stop to this after his easy dismissal last weekend, but shit, my pussy doesn't want me to. I hear him unzip his pants, and it gets me even more heated. Within seconds, I feel his dick rub against my ass, and I'm dripping for it.

"Pleaseeee," I beg. The wait is unbearable.

"That just happens to be the magic word, sweetheart." He leans me forward and rubs my pussy from behind. His hand is soaked in my juices. He coats my ass with these juices, and I immediately tighten. I suspect where this is leading. When I feel the head of his cock at my entrance back there, I know that I'm correct. I've never been taken there. It's the one place that has remained mine. "Relax and let me inside, Harlow. Let me be the first. Let me claim this ass."

How did he know it is uncharted territory? At this moment, I want to be sexually liberated. It's not like it's some sacred act I need to save for marriage. I'm tainted goods anyway. I may regret this in the morning when he goes back to ignoring me, but tonight I'm owning my sexuality. I say when and how. It's up to me, and I want to be fucked by this sexy as hell rock god.

Phoenix

I WATCH AS INDECISION WAGES WITHIN HER THOUGHTS. I want her to be sure about what she is about to give me. I don't think she realizes this is the first real test of her submission to me. This is a pivotal point. If she agrees, she is giving me something that she has never shared with anyone else. Her reaction to my dick being in such proximity with her ass clued me into its virginal status. She had the same reaction last time we fucked. I could have had the pussy by now, and we could have already been out of here to meet the guys, but I don't want that. I want her submission, and I want her to give it to me. This act will prove that she's surrendered her mind and her body to my will.

I thought I could stay away from her. I wanted to. Then she came in here tonight in a dress so out of character for her, and I couldn't resist. Not because she looks sexy as fuck, because that is undebatable, but because that in itself was a hint at her ability to submit—her readiness. She wanted to get my attention—needed to show me she can be desirable. There is no question that she wasn't into those dickfaces. The show was for me. The fact that she stepped so far out of her comfort zone for my benefit shows that she was willing to put what she thought I deemed appealing over her own comfort.

I'M SELFISH IN THAT I CAN'T IGNORE THE SIGNS, YET I'M not a complete asshole to take advantage of her vulnerability. I don't think she even recognizes this trait in herself. It fucking made my dick so hard on stage, I wanted to jump off stage and fuck this shit out of her that instant. Even now, a bead of cum forms at the tip of my dick. I mix it with her wetness already pooling around her asshole. I think I'll burst from the anticipation when she gives me a timid nod, giving me the green light. There is no putting the fucking demons away now.

"Hell, yes," I say in approval. "No clenching, sweetheart. Just push out as I push in." I slip a condom from my pocket and roll it over my dick. I wet it with some of my saliva before repositioning myself at her entrance. I don't have any KY jelly handy, so our body's natural lubricant will have to suffice. Upon insertion, there is a slight flinch, but I tighten my grip on her hip. "Relax," I encourage soothingly.

I use one hand to reach around and massage her clit. As she begins to wiggle in my arms, I know it is the distraction she needs. She pushes back toward me, and I use the opportunity to slide in farther. When I'm more than halfway in, I pause to tease her further. I place little kisses along the back of her neck.

"Uhhhhhhh," she moans incoherently.

I PUSH FARTHER UNTIL I'M IN TO THE HILT. "ARE YOU okay?"

"Yes," she says breathily. I'm sure the alcohol is working in my favor.

"I'm going to move now, babe." She nods her head, and I pull out slightly before pushing my way back in. Fuck, her tightness feels so damn good. I give her a few more slow strokes to make sure that she is acclimated to the size of my dick. When I can tell she is getting into it, I increase my rhythm. I grab both hips now as I slam into her. "Your ass feels amazing, Harlow. Fuuuuuuck," I groan. I can feel a tightness in my balls already. I'm not going to last much longer. I need her to get there. I finger her pussy as I drive into her ass.

"Phoenix," she moans, and I know that she is close. I find her G-spot and her floodgates open. Holy hell, she comes all over my hand, and it is such a turn-on. I fuck her faster until I reach my own orgasm. My dick throbs in her, and I know that this can't be the last time. My three-time fuck rule has vanished with her. She has appealed to my demons. Now, I have to have her. Although I'm not changing my mind about not wanting a relationship, I'm willing to loosen some of my rules to give in to her temptation. She has submitted to me, and I want to expose and share my kink with her.

She has no idea the door she just opened. We savor the moment for a few seconds before I slide out of her. I lead her to a restroom, here inside the storage room. I turn the water on and grab a few paper towels to moisten before handing her a few. These will have to do. We can't both go back to the truck smelling like sex. I'm sure Asher is wondering where we are by now, but I couldn't wait another second without answering the submission she had unknowingly given. Once we got back to the house, it would have been too late.

Harlow shyly turns her back to me, to shield my view of her cleaning herself up. I have my work cut out for me, breaking down the rest of those walls, but I'm definitely up for it. I let her be for now, though. I wash up the best I can with water alone and tuck my dick back into my jeans. When she's done, I lead her back out into the club. No words are spoken as we make our way to the truck.

"There you two are. Where have you been? I thought I was going to have to come in after you," Asher says.

"Harlow got a little sick and needed to pray to the porcelain god for a bit," I lie. She shoots me a look of disbelief. Her eyebrows knit before she schools her face to play along.

"Yeah. I'm feeling a lot better now," she adds.

"You're going to have to slow down on the drinking, sis. Don't drink so much that you make yourself sick," Asher chastises.

"I'm fine, Asher," she assures. She narrows her eyes at me, and I smirk. Better that little lie than me tell him what his baby sister was really getting into.

"So how did it go?" Irelyn asks as she joins us outside. I would have thought she would have beaten us out here.

"Don't know yet," Ren speaks up. "Desiree told us that she enjoyed our performance and that she would be in touch by Sunday."

"Yeah, but she stayed for the entire show, so that's something," Killian offers.

"I think you guys have this in the bag. You gave so much variety and really showed your range of style as artists," Irelyn says. Harlow nods her head in agreement. I sure hope so. This is what we have been working toward. I can't thank Sevyn enough for the connection.

"I didn't think you guys were paying much attention. You were so wrapped up in those college shits."

"Are you kidding me?" Harlow speaks up. "We have ears and eyes. You were doing a pretty good job yourself of being wrapped up in skankville row." Jealousy and disdain drip from her sarcasm, and I have to work hard to contain my laughter. It is almost too cute.

"Skankville row?" I seek to clarify, although I'm sure I know the women she is referring to. They're my most loyal fans.

"You know. The thirsty women who are always front and center," she confirms. "Skankville row." I can't help it. I laugh my ass off, and the guys join in on the laughter.

"That's awesome," Killian amuses. "Haven't you fucked like all of them?" I swear Killian doesn't know when to shut the fuck up sometimes.

"No, I haven't, dipshit. And you fuckers have tapped some of that, so shut it. Why are we even discussing groupie fucks in the midst of these women, anyway? I'm sure they don't want to hear that shit." I look over at Harlow, and her face is tight. She is probably already regretting her decision to let me fuck her again. Gah, this motherfucker is ruining my shit. I'm going to have to work that much harder to get her to give in to her submissive nature.

"Yeah, really classy," Harlow says, rolling her eyes. She gets in the truck, and Killian falls silent as he realizes his mistake.

The ride home is full of discussion about tonight's gig and speculation on our chances of landing a record deal with Pretty Boy Rock. I can see the girls talking quietly among themselves. I don't know if I'll have a chance to get Harlow alone again before I have to leave in the morning. I have something to take care of again, and I'm sure Asher will be taking them back before I return. Even so, I'm glad we had tonight. She's been on my mind since last weekend. The way things ended that morning was unsettling.

My thoughts have cycled through various instances of leaving her the hell alone and introducing her to my brand of kink. I know that I'm not good for her, yet the selfish part of me can't find a reason to let that stop me. I thought I had time on my side to maybe fuck her out of my system, but that one taste was addicting. When Asher announced that she was coming to the show tonight, I knew the task of staying away from her would be challenging. Seeing her tonight in that dress and owning the room made the decision for me. I've never felt so out of control. My reaction to her needed to be addressed. This was submission in its rawest form. It called to my repressed nature in a way that left me powerless to fight it any longer.

I can't give her a relationship or promise of more. There will be no illusions of happily ever after, but I can introduce her to what she doesn't even know she's craving, my dominance. The question is, can she handle what I'm prepared to offer? My dick twitches in my jeans at just the thought. This should be interesting. Now to determine the best way to tell her she is a submissive and what that means. We finally arrive back at the house, and I use the last opportunity to get a word in to her. As she climbs out of the truck, I quickly whisper in her ear.

"We need to talk," I say.

CHAPTER EIGHTEEN
Harlow

I could barely sleep last night. My last encounter with Phoenix, along with his ominous statement that we need to talk, was on constant replay. I'm back in the room where I spent this past summer, and all the memories flood my mind, including my first run-in with Phoenix in the shower. I look over at Irelyn, who is still knocked out next to me, even though it is well after nine a.m. I guess my body just has an aversion to sleeping in. I decide to get up and grab a couple of cups of coffee. The soreness of my ass as I walk down the stairs reminds me that last night did very much happen.

"Morning, Harlow," Phoenix says from the kitchen. He is leaning against the counter, waiting for the Keurig to finish brewing his cup of coffee.

"Morning," I say, waiting for the ball to drop. What is he going to tell me? "Where is everyone?" I ask, looking around. The house is too quiet.

"Either sleeping in or already left." The Keurig stops, so he grabs his mug and empties the chamber of the used k-cup. "All yours," he offers while gesturing toward the coffeemaker. Why is he drawing this out? Apparently, he needs to tell me something, so why hasn't he brought it up yet?

"What did you want to tell me, Phoenix?"

"What do you mean?" He genuinely looks confused. His eyebrows knit together in question.

"Last night, when we got back, you said we needed to talk." He thinks it over for a second and scratches his head.

"Oh well, I don't remember at the moment." He moves aside and lets me brew my coffee. He is different today somehow. I've experienced his hot and cold before. I must say that I'm not a fan.

"Look, if it's about what happened last night, don't sweat it. It was fun, and now it's over. You don't have to worry about making things awkward." Phoenix walks over to me, and I'm not ready for his response. He cups my face and kisses me slow and passionately. There is no hesitation or teasing like he normally does. This kiss is unlike the others. I feel that he is trying to express himself this way, but I have no idea what it means. I wrap my arms around his neck, and he deepens the kiss. He palms my ass and brings me closer to him. I don't miss the bulge in his jeans.

"Shut up," he finally says, breaking the kiss. "Get out of your head."

"What does this mean, Phoenix?" I don't want to push or have expectations, but I'm not a mind reader. What are we doing? What does he want from me?

"Uhhh, I have to go, Harlow. We'll talk later. I can't answer that right now." He takes a huge sip of his coffee before he jets in the direction of the door. So, he's running again. *What the fuck?* One thing is for certain. We do need to talk. He can't keep screwing with my emotions.

I MARCH UPSTAIRS AND GRAB MY PHONE. PHOENIX GAVE me his number right before I moved to the dorms, but I have never had a reason to call him. I think this warrants a phone call. His phone goes straight to voicemail. *Shit.* I'm not willing to give up, though. I need answers, so I know what I need to do. Later, when Asher gets ready to bring us back, I can't go. Irelyn will have to go back alone. Phoenix will have to bring me back tonight or tomorrow, but I'm not leaving here without answers. I don't want to spend all week trying to figure out his cryptic messages and indecisiveness.

∽

WHEN PHOENIX GETS BACK TO THE HOUSE, HE IS stunned to see me sitting on the sofa. He looks around before walking over to me.

"What are you still doing here?" He looks at his watch. It's just after two. "Asher told me he was bringing you and Irelyn home around noon."

"Yes, he left to take Irelyn home about an hour ago." I fidget because I know this is it. I can't chicken out.

"Well, why didn't you leave with them? What's going on?" He lowers his voice. "Where is everyone else?"

"They're all gone. I stayed because we need to have that talk. The kiss this morning was confusing and unfair. I feel like you're taking me on a ride I didn't agree to get on." I watch as he clenches his fist and his face hardens.

"Kiss?" Okay, so tough shit. He doesn't like me bringing up the kiss. Maybe it was a moment of weakness for him, but it shows even more why we need to talk.

"Okay, forget the kiss. Last night you said we needed to talk. What did you mean by that?" His face relaxes, and he runs a hand through his hair.

"Honestly, I didn't think we'd be having this conversation today. Thought you'd be gone." He takes a seat next to me and rests his elbows on his knees. He laces his fingers together and then finally looks over at me. "Be sure you want to know what you're asking," he warns.

"I'm tired of tap dancing around the unknown. What the hell are we doing, Phoenix?"

"Well, princess, I thought we were fucking, but what

do you call it?" He smirks, and I swear I just want to smack the sarcasm right out of him.

"Okay, I see this was pointless." I stayed for nothing. He's not going to be serious. He just wants to string me along. Damn him, if he thinks I'm just going to serve up the ass the next time he gets the urge to mess with me again. I'm halfway standing when he uses one hand to push me back onto the sofa.

"Sit down, Harlow. You want answers...just remember you asked for them. I won't sugarcoat shit."

"I didn't ask you to." We stare at each other for what seems like an eternity before he breaks the silence.

"You're a submissive," he says bluntly. He stares at me expectantly, waiting for my reaction. *What the fuck?*

"What the hell are you talking about? No, I'm not." What kind of crack is he smoking, because surely he's tripping or high or whatever the fuck crack does to you.

"Do you even know what it means to have a submissive nature?" He quizzes me like it's supposed to fucking matter. I'm not that. I roll my eyes. See that. That eye roll means fuck you, I voice internally.

"It means some freaky kink shit, where you get off on the guy telling you what to do, and if you don't listen, he gets to beat the shit out of you until you conform. No, thank you." He is biting his lip, obviously trying to keep from laughing at me. "What-the fuck-ever. I'm not one of those 'please spank my ass and make me listen, Sir' kind of bitches." Holy shit. The other night...in the storage room... he said, Sir. He was trying to get me to say, "Yes, Sir." Stop the fucking presses. Is he trying to tell me now that he is a dominant? *Wait.* And the song about him having demons. *Holy shitballs.*

"I see the wheels turning, princess. Say it." I scoot over a tad away from him. Does he want to beat me? "Your analysis of what it means to be submissive is wrong, by the way. Women read too many romance novels. That shit isn't real life." It's his turn to roll his eyes.

"So you're a Dooommm?" I stutter.

"Dominant," he finishes for me. "I am, I guess, but not in the traditional sense. My tastes are somewhat modified, and I don't practice this on a regular basis. I'm very selective and very private, so I don't go to BDSM clubs or anything remotely similar. There are varying degrees to the term, but yes, I like control. I'm different in that I don't spank women—not to inflict pain anyway. I happen to like slapping your ass. It's just so inviting and curvaceous. No, there are other means for me to deliver punishment if I deem it fitting, but there is no need for the most part. The acts I partake in are consensual. The woman wants to submit—hence never forced or coerced. If a woman doesn't want what I want, I walk away, simple as that." My mouth falls open with all that I have just learned about him. I have to say. I never saw that one coming. I just thought he was a manwhore.

"But we didn't do any of that control stuff you're talking about." I have to say my curiosity has been piqued. How has he hidden this about himself? I would have never guessed.

"Exactly. You weren't ready. I don't share this part of myself with every woman I fuck."

"Sheesh. Why not? You consider it some sort a gift. Some sort of privilege." Give me a break.

"Something like that," Phoenix admits. I'm baffled. "That is not a part of me that I share willingly. It's my dark place, and not everyone is equipped to handle that side of me or deserves to know something so personal about me. If it's going to be a quick rocks-off session, why bother? They won't be around long enough for me to care to indulge."

HEARING HIM TALK ABOUT FUCKING SOMEONE ELSE stings a bit. I don't want to picture that shit. "So how does any of this make me a submissive?" I want to get back to his first accusation. How did he arrive at such an asinine conclusion?

"It doesn't. The two are independent of one another. My tendencies have nothing to do with yours. I just recognize the trait because I am a dominant." He turns and places one knee on the sofa. He is facing me now, and I can't escape his scrutiny. He is watching my every move —my reaction to whatever it is he is about to tell me. "A D/s relationship is about power exchange, but a submissive is not powerless or weak. The submissive willing submits because she trusts that she will be taken care of. You'd be surprised to learn how many powerful women, executive types, practice the lifestyle. The relinquishing of responsibility can be liberating. The woman's willingness to submit is her power."

"Again, what does that have to do with me?"

"From the moment we met, there was a connection. I think subconsciously our inner needs recognized the traits in one another. That first day, you conceded to letting me keep my things in the closet of your room and to sharing the master bath with me, although there were other bathrooms in the house."

"That's only because I didn't want to be a bitch and make you find a place for all of your shit after I just took the room that was once yours. Also we were the only two bedrooms upstairs. Why would I insist you use a different bathroom than the one upstairs with us? It's called compromise." How in the hell did he make that inference? So I must be a submissive because I let him keep his shit in my room and was willing to share a bathroom?

"Then there was the shower incident. You stood there, frozen in place, and watched me shower. You could not move because I had affected you at that moment. Without trying, I had control. Just briefly, but it was there. I just didn't make the connection until thinking back on it last night." I laugh, but he just stares at me.

"You are quite delusional." *Add that to your repertoire — manwhore, dominant, and delusional.*

"Hmm. Then it was the change in your clothing. You started with the baggiest shit ever known to man. It may be simply coincidental, but after our run-in with you getting out of the shower and conversation of how beautiful you were, things changed. You didn't need the clothes or the makeup that you were hiding behind. You subconsciously submitted to my wishes." If my eyes bug out any further, I think they'll pop out of my head.

"Just wow." It's the only coherent thought I can form at the moment. "Irelyn is the one. You know what? Never mind. I don't believe any of that."

"I can think of several instances, now that I'm thinking about them, but I won't explore them all," he continues, like I haven't said anything. "Your last and final acts of submission was at the club last night. Contrary to your extreme need to be covered, you wore the skimpiest piece of fabric one could get away with and still call it a dress. Of course, it was for my benefit—you needed to get my attention. You were seeking my approval, my desire, per se. It made my cock so hard during my whole performance. I knew I had to fuck you. I had to give you a taste of what you were asking for." His eyes are hooded now as he recalls our romp session in the storage room.

"If all that isn't proof enough, you gave me the most precious gift. I say precious; because it is something that you have never given to another, yet you gave to me so freely. You let me claim your ass, literally, in a final act of submission that erased all doubt for me." I don't know what to say. Yes, some of the things he said have some merit, but that doesn't make me a submissive. It makes me a woman who is ready to explore her sexuality, after believing for so long that this feat wasn't possible.

"Phoenix. You have your perceptions and idealizations about the reasons for my behavior. I can't change that. You're entitled to your opinion. The question is, what are we doing? You're so hot and cold. One minute you're dismissing me, without so much as a word or explanation, and the next minute you're fucking me in the ass in a storage room. I'm not just a piece ass for you to fuck between groupies when you're bored, or simply when the mood strikes because you think you recognize some submissive behavior from me." There I said it. I didn't let my traitorous body keep me from getting my point across.

"I'm not looking for a relationship, Harlow. I won't be your boyfriend. I can't give you that. I would be lying if I said I didn't want to explore a D/s relationship with you. In that, I won't sleep with anyone else. We would be exclusive."

"I'm not looking to be your kinky sex slave, Phoenix." He throws his head back and belts out a hearty laugh. It's so contagious that I can't help but join in.

We've gotten into a serious topic here, yet he is able to lighten it with a simple laugh.

"Absolutely not, princess. Let me show you a side of me that so few get to see. I promise you unimaginable pleasure. I will introduce you to things that will make your body sing. You can refuse or change your mind at any time. I'm not into pain, so you don't have to worry about that. Mostly just a release of control and allowing me to introduce you to some things." The look in his eyes is hopeful. I can't believe I'm even considering this, but he said I could refuse anything or change my mind. I'm somewhat afraid, but I want the pleasure he promises. I want to take back my power by my decision to give it to someone. It will be my sexual experience, to be of my free will, and not decided for me.

"Do I need a safe word?" I look down at my intertwined knuckles. Phoenix cups my chin and makes me look up at him.

"We will discuss beforehand the things I want to try with you, so you can tell me if anything is a hard stop. If you decide to try it and don't like it, then you simply tell me to stop, or in some cases, dig your nails in my arm." Why would I dig my nails into him? Or do I even want to know? "I don't want to talk about safe words right now, though, because my dick is already getting hard and ready to play. Unfortunately, I know the guys should be back any moment now because we're supposed to hear from Desiree by four today. It turns out that we don't have to wait until Sunday," he finishes.

CHAPTER NINETEEN
Phoenix

"So am I to assume your inquisition on safe words means you're saying yes?" I ask. I said I didn't want to talk about it, but it's useless. I know the answer, but I need her to say the words. Verbalization of her understanding of this arrangement we're about to enter.

"What are you proposing? A D/s relationship where we explore your world of kink and be sexually exclusive, minus any romantic relationship? Did I just about sum it up?" I can't get a read on how Harlow feels about this proposal, but she is correct.

"It's all I'm capable of offering. I'm not looking for a girlfriend or any false expectations of things leading to more. I want to fuck you in ways that will ruin your vanilla mentality and have your pussy aching for me. I can be faithful to the arrangement, but I won't be yours in the romantic sense. If you catch feelings, all of this will end.

I'm sorry, I don't want a relationship with anyone." Harlow gets up and walks over to stare out of the window. I have to be honest from the beginning. I don't believe in trickery or playing with a woman's heart. She has to be in this for the right reasons. I don't know if I'm capable of loving or being loved, so I'd rather not start down a path that leads to disappointment. Things are safer this way. No expectations equal zero disappointments. I am, however, willing to give her the best of me, if she lets me. My sins. My darkness. My demons. They define who I am and, at present, the best I can offer, hence the best of me.

"Okay," she says so lightly, I'm unsure if I heard her correctly.

"Okay, what?" I get up and walk over to the window where she is standing. She turns around and looks me directly in the eyes.

"Sir. Okay, Sir." I can't believe my fucking ears. That is not what I was implying or expecting her to say. I was merely trying to get a clear answer of agreement of our arrangement. Those words coming from her mouth is music to my ears. My cock is at full attention now. She looks down, entering into submission mode. I lift her chin because that is not what I want. I put her hand over the hardness of my jeans, so she can feel how happy she has made me.

"You see what you do to me?" I'm milliseconds from saying to hell with it and bending her over right here when I hear the door downstairs. The guys are back. *Dammit.* "You're safe for now. But later—" I cut my sentence short as Killian is the first one upstairs. Harlow leaves out the door onto the deck. I'm guessing to hide that blush I've put on her face.

"Have you heard from Desiree yet?" Ren asks, following Killian.

"Not yet." I look up at the clock. It's twenty past the hour. Her call is late. "Don't worry. She'll call." I don't want to worry, but I'm curious as to why we haven't heard anything. What if the executives said no? This would be a major disappointment for the guys.

"What if they've decided not to bring us on?" Killian asks, echoing my thoughts.

"Then we keep trying. Pretty Boy Rock is a huge upcoming record label, but if they don't sign us, then it's their loss." The door opens and closes downstairs—Asher's back. I might as well find something to watch on the TV, I hate this waiting shit. Patience is not a virtue for me.

"Look who I found outside," Asher announces as he enters the room. It's Desiree. My heart speeds up as I jump off the sofa.

"Hello, guys. Sorry, I'm late. That traffic was monstrous, but I didn't want to deliver the news over the phone." That has to be good news, right? Surely, she wouldn't have driven all this way just to tell us no. Asher waves at Harlow to summon her to join us. Desiree heads to our dining table and sets down a briefcase. She has the tightest dress on. I can't see how she can breathe, let alone walk. I see the lust in the eyes of the guys with every step she takes in her stilettos. She swings her hips, not sure if it's her natural switch, or if she is putting on an enticing show for us. Even Asher's nose is open, and he has a woman who he is seeing at the moment. That long-distance shit is for the birds. Still, I'm not even tempted. I just want the news. Is this the moment that changes our lives forever?

"Not a problem. We're glad that you made it. Unexpected, but a pleasant surprise," I assure.

"Glad to hear it because I have some good news," Desiree comments. My ears perk up, and the guys move in closer to the table as she continues, "Our label wants to sign you guys."

"Hell, yes!" Asher woots.

"Oh, man. How does this work? When do we start?"

"Well, I've been assigned to manage you guys. Please understand that you won't start as the main act. You guys have only a few of your own original tracks, and you don't have a substantial following outside the clubs you play." I expected that we would have to put in the work. We're ready to do what it takes. "We would start by having you guys be the opening act for Wild Silence."

"Holy shit." I can barely contain my surprise. Those

guys are fucking huge. I admire their sound, and their story is similar to ours in respect to how they got started.

"Yeah. They're pretty huge," Desiree says, reading my mind. "Their tour stops are always sold out and guaranteed to get you guys the exposure you need. You'll play your original music, but you will need to get in the studio to record more. We can discuss the logistics later about a producer and possible co-writer. We don't want to change your sound." Desiree opens the briefcase on the table and shuffles through some files.

"What are the numbers?" I ask. I'm the spokesperson for our band. It all sounds great, but the dollars have to make sense for us.

I KNOW WE HAVE TO PROVE OURSELVES FIRST BEFORE WE can expect a huge payout, but a contract needs to stipulate a percentage with progression as we make a name in the industry. Desiree looks over at Harlow, who has been quiet up to this point. It is obvious that she doesn't want to disclose our figures in front of her.

"I'll just step outside," Harlow says, apparently also feeling the vibe. "Congrats, guys. You deserve it."

"Thank you," Killian and Ren say in unison. I just nod my thanks.

"I'll be out there in a second," Asher tells her. She waves her hand slightly and disappears out onto the deck. Desiree waits until she is both out of earshot and sight before she continues.

"The label is prepared to offer you guys fifteen percent, and that's pretty generous. The industry standard is thirteen. The breakdown is that the label gets sixty percent because they carry all the upfront costs of getting you guys produced and promoted. Distribution gets twenty percent and ensures that your album is released everywhere, as well as optimal radio time." Desiree lays out a pie graph that outlines how our pay is broken down.

"So our lawyer, producer, and managers get paid out of our twenty percent?" She nods in the affirmative. "Why do we need two managers?"

"Well, as your business manager, I get five percent. If you act as the personal manager for your group, you can filter some of the percentage among your band and take a greater percentage for yourself." The guys all agree this would be the fair thing to do.

"YOU GUYS WILL GET A MILLION-DOLLAR ADVANCE UP front to record your album, pay the expenses we just discussed, and for tour support." I can't find anything wrong with this deal. As she stated, it all seems legit and fair, not to mention generous. She steps outside briefly with Harlow, for us to discuss, but it doesn't take us long to deliberate. This is our blessing. The guys get choked up over the million dollars, but I remind them of the breakdown. They need me, Mr. Control Freak, in charge. I'm logical and will be frugal as fuck when it comes to our band. There will be no fucking off the money. We summon Desiree back in, and Harlow returns with her.

"One last question." The guys look at me like I've grown a second head. In their mind, it's a done deal. It is, I just have one more question. "When will be starting to tour? Oh, and we're keeping the name Phoenix Rising."

"Legitimate question," Desiree surmises. "Of course you'll be keeping your name. It's badass. Your tour will start at the beginning of January. That gives you guys a couple of months to perfect the songs you already have written and get them professionally recorded. Maybe pick one of them as your first single. It will also allow time to at least start on some new material to sample while on tour." She smiles and hands me a pen as she pushes the contract in my direction. "I will need a signature from each of you if you're on board."

"We are." I smile back. My day has been made, first with Harlow and now this. I know our lives will be changed forever. I lean over the table and proudly sign my name to the piece of paper that is the evidence of everything we've worked hard for.

Once Desiree has all of our signatures, she shakes our hands. "Welcome aboard," she congratulates. "I look forward to managing you guys. I know we're going to do some wonderful things. Can you all come down this weekend to meet the executives? I know you have a regular gig at Club Luxe, and this is short notice."

"Sure. I'll talk to Steve today. He'll understand. He wanted this for us. He knew there would be some conflicts with our schedule to play there in pursuit of our dreams." I will never forget what he did for us. Club Luxe will always be our home.

"Great! I want to take you guys out on Saturday. We'll get dinner, and then we'll hit Excalibur. The club is owned by the senior VP of Pretty Boy Rock, so we'll get the VIP treatment." She winks. The guys woot and howl their excitement. It's been a while since we've been to a club just to party because we always have a gig on the weekend. As long as it's on the label's dime, I'm game. This very well just may be our last time to unwind, since we're going to have to step our game up. Our schedule is about to get really hectic.

"Looking forward to it." I shake Desiree's hand one last time before she leaves. I turn to look at the guys. I don't want to wait until the weekend to celebrate. I'm thinking a nice low-key dinner and drinks are in order. "What do you guys say to us going out and celebrating, now that it's official? Nothing major—just dinner and drinks."

"I'm game for it. We can save the partying until this weekend," Killian suggests.

"Yeah. Like our last hoorah," Ren adds. This is why we

mesh so well. None of us are into drugs and major partying. Don't get me wrong; we are far from saints. We just have always put the needs of the band first. We're not your stereotypical definition of a rock band. We do love pussy, though, and will indulge in that shit. We named ourselves Phoenix Rising for this very reason. Still, the band comes first.

"Come on. Let's do this," Asher says, slapping me on the back. "Are you coming, Harlow?" She hasn't said much, and I wonder what she is thinking. I'm going to have to find time this week to go and see her, so we can explore our arrangement. In light of our record deal, I don't know how much time we will have, but I'm definitely ready to fuck the shit out of her. My balls ache just thinking about it.

"No, you guys go ahead. This is your day. I can wait here until you get back if you all are going now," she says.

"Nonsense. But I will take you back to the dorm if you're ready," Asher speaks up. I want to volunteer, so I can solidify a plan for this week. Then again, that would be just plain torture not to be able to have her now. Besides, I don't want to raise sudden suspicion. The guys know that I'm not that generous. My reputation with the extent of my relationship with women is quite tainted. Instead, I watch as she nods in agreement and gives us a small wave goodbye. She looks at me briefly, but I'm unable to communicate that I will be in contact. She leaves with Asher, and I'm forced to wait until she gets back to her dorm. I will call her and set this fuckship in motion.

Harlow

When I get back to the dorms, Irelyn is out. I know she will have plenty of questions for me, so I appreciate the reprieve. I need some time to reflect on my conversation with Phoenix. I'm still reeling in shock to learn that he considers himself a dominant. I'm still unsure of what all that means. What does he want me to do? What does he want to do with me? My mind has cycled through several scenarios and possibilities on the way here. Asher had asked why I was so quiet. Now that I'm alone with my thoughts, the nerves have kicked in. I want this with him. I want to try. I must admit it sounds exciting to release control, but scary at the same time. Can I do it? I wasn't forthcoming with him about my past. I have secrets that I haven't disclosed to anyone. Still, I want this. I need this. For so long, I've hidden behind the makeup and baggy clothes. I was afraid of a man to see me. I was afraid of intimacy. The change in clothes and makeup was the first step at normalcy for me. Owning my sexuality is logically the next step.

I can't worry about where this music career will take Phoenix. The guys will be going on tour soon, so I know that will end whatever we are about to embark on. As long as I remember that this is just a fuck and the chance to explore my sexuality, I'll be fine. I will enjoy it while it lasts. He will be my stepping-stone in preparation for the next man who comes along.

My phone rings, and I smile when I see that it is Phoenix. I wonder if he is anticipating our hook up like I am.

"Hello," I answer, feigning indifference.

"Hey, princess." I have to admit the fact that he calls me that is growing on me. It's quite different from when Asher says it—a naughty undertone that is kind of hot. "Glad to see you made it home. Have you been thinking about our discussion?"

"Nope. Just pulled out my books to study," I fib. I can't let on that is all I have been able to think about since I left. I lie across my bed and cup the phone closer to my ear. I'm glad Irelyn is not here to see this cheesy ass grin on my face. His voice is just so sexy over the phone. I can't explain why he has the ability to turn me into a mush of hormones.

"Lies," he accuses. "I bet you're wet right now. You have FaceTime, don't you?"

"Yes," I answer hesitantly. Where is he going with this? "Why?"

"Mmm, I want to see."

"See what?" My voice raises an octave in surprise. My

heart slams against my chest. I know it has something to do with exposing myself.

"I want to see how wet your pussy is for me. How turned on you are just thinking about everything I've told you." His voice is husky now, and I recognize the change. He is every bit of turned on as I am. He is right. I'm soaking, but I'm too chickenshit to show him. Both encounters with him have been in the dark: my fears hidden in the shadows—a way for me to be brave.

CHAPTER TWENTY

Harlow

Holy crap! What was I thinking? How did I ever think I could do this? Liberation, my ass. I don't think I can go from totally covered and hiding, to naked and bare for him without a way to hide my insecurities.

"Phoenix—" I begin, but he cuts me off.

"Don't sweat it. I don't need the visual proof. It's in the voice. It tells me all that I need to know. From the slight hitch of your breath to the hesitation in your speech, I know I affect you. You're ready for my cock, and that is all that matters. I'm going to fuck the shyness right out you, princess. There will be no more room left for preservation—only lust, want, and lack inhibition," he promises. "That tingling you're feeling right now. That's your pussy agreeing with me. It wants everything I have to offer. She's the brave one. She's the one who responds to me when you're too afraid to. She and I will be getting well acquainted."

I squeeze my legs together because he is right. The ache between my legs is downright unbearable. His forwardness is raw and speaks to "her," just as he predicted.

"Umm, okay." Gah, I can hear the quiver in my own voice. "So when are we going to see each other?" Not too obvious, right? Especially since I really want to ask, "When do you plan on getting acquainted with her?" He chuckles on the other end of the phone because he sees right through my subliminal question.

"What time do you get out of class on Wednesday?"

"Monday and Wednesdays are my light days, so I'll be done before noon." I'm going to have to think of something tell Irelyn. I can't divulge the truth. She will just try to talk me out of it—insist that he is using me. She doesn't know my past, so she wouldn't be able to fathom why I need this. Our last plan was to make Phoenix jealous of how he dismissed me so easily, last time we fucked. She will think I'm absolutely crazy for giving him a chance to do it again.

"Perfect. I can pick you up by one. We can grab lunch and get the same hotel."

"Okay." Tension builds, as I'm more concerned about how I'm going to explain my disappearance. I don't want to have to lie to her, yet it is all I seem to be doing lately.

"I want you to do something for me before I let you off the phone." His voice takes on an even huskier vibrato. I'm scared to ask.

"What is that?" I ask anyway.

"I want you to unbutton those jeans you're wearing and slide your hand into your panties," he instructs. *What the?* I look toward the door. Irelyn could come in at any minute. "Now, princess." Damn. The command is sharp, but not offensive. This is it: the beginning of his control. He can't see me, so I could pretend, but I need to use his absence as practice. I've touched myself before—not often, but I've done it.

I UNBUTTON MY JEANS AND SLIDE MY HAND INTO MY underwear as instructed. "Now what?"

"Run your middle finger along your clit. Feel the slickness there. With each pass, allow your finger to move deeper toward your pussy. Stroke yourself for me, baby." My finger has already started to move on its accord. If Irelyn bursts in here at this moment, she is in for a show. I try to stave off the moans trying to escape my throat. These walls are thin. "Fucking let me hear you, Harlow. I want to hear you as you come for me." My fingers are sliding between my folds even faster now, as I work my clit from the sound of his voice. I'm so close.

"I cannnnnnnn't Phoenix," I let out breathily. The

whole freaking dorm will hear me. I bite my lip to suppress my urge to let it out. The wet sounds of my pussy as I stroke faster fill the air of the room.

"Fuck. I can hear it," he groans. "I can hear how wet your pussy is. Shit, that makes me wish I was there to slide my dick so deep into you and pound the fucking moans right out of you—have you screaming my name." That does it. My legs shake as I coat my fingers with my cum. I can't speak. I bite the pillow, as my orgasm seems to roll on and on. I can hear his heavy breathing as I lay here incapacitated by the strongest orgasm I've ever achieved by myself. That was fucking intense.

"Shit. That..." I can't even describe it.

"Hmmm, that good, huh? You needed that release. You were wound too tight after our talk this afternoon. I didn't want you to have to wait until Wednesday. Just wait until you see what I have in store you." He can be so cryptic. I slide my hand out my underwear but I still can't move, so I just lay here in savor mode.

"What about you?"

"What about me?"

"What about your release?" Apparently, my orgasmic state has made me bold for the moment.

"Oh. I think I'll save it all for you. So be ready." *Jesus.* This escalated quickly. "For now, have a hot shower and get some rest. There will be no time for sleeping for what I have in mind."

"Really now." I smile lazily. I can feel my eyes growing heavy. I'm spent, but I know I need to get up and shower. I'm sure I smell like sex.

"Oh. You'll see. I don't bluff. Night, Harlow."

"Night," I whisper, but he has already clicked off. I drag my ass out of bed to find something sleep in before heading down the hall to shower. I don't know where Irelyn is, but she and I need to talk tomorrow. I'm too tired to wait up for her tonight. I'm going to shower and call it an early night. I'm not sure what I'm going to tell her yet, but I definitely need to tell her something before Wednesday. I let the hot water rain down on me as I reminisce on what just happened. Phoenix has shown himself. He is so much more than I originally thought—more dangerous, to be exact.

∽

I WAKE UP FEELING HOT. NOT TURNED ON. No literally hot from body heat. The room is completely dark, but from the limbs draped across my lower legs, I would say Irelyn has decided to crash in my bed. Again. Her bed has so much crap on it. I shove her until I can untangle myself, and she grumbles.

"What time is it?" I can feel her searching around the bed. Luckily this bed is at least full size compared to her twin. "I can't find my phone."

"Ugh. Move over." I reach under my pillow and grab mine. "It's a little after six in the morning, pyscho. Why can't you sleep in your own bed?" I say, only half kidding.

"Because your bed is bigger and mine has stuff on it," she points out like it's the most logical explanation.

"You said I could have the bigger bed. Besides, if you had this one, you'd just have more crap on it."

"True." She stumbles out of bed and feels around the wall until she finds the light switch. It really sucks not having any windows in here. You can never tell what time of day it is. "Get up, biotch. I have a lot to tell you." I cover my head up, knowing I'm going to get up. The funny thing is, I have a lot to tell her too.

"What?" I say from underneath the covers. She walks over and yanks them down before she flops next to me.

"I FUCKED MIKE LAST NIGHT," SHE BLURTS OUT. "YOU were supposed to go with me to that house party, " she adds.

"I'm glad I didn't now. I would have just been a third wheel, or worse, James would have gotten ideas and would've been sadly disappointed." This doesn't surprise me about Irelyn. She is such a free spirit. If she is feeling you, she goes with it. She doesn't put on any false pretenses of innocence. If she wants to fuck, she fucks. Sometimes she tells me that she will never talk to the guy again, that she just wanted a sample. Her behavior is worse than a guy's sometimes.

"Well, how was it? Do you think you'll see him again?"

"It was okay. It wasn't epic. We were both tipsy as shit. We were at his frat house, so we were lucky not to be interrupted. If he asks me out, I'd consider it. If not, no love loss." She goes on and on about the party, who all showed up, and told me all about the gossip surrounding one of the sorority girls, who is rumored to be stalking one of the frat guys' girlfriends. I yawn and try to keep up with it all. I'm so glad I missed it all. Not my kind of crowd at all. "So what happened with the guys? Did they get the record deal?"

I run down all the details as I remember them. "They have a couple of months before they go on the road," I add. I suspect that she has a crush on Killian. She always perks up when he's around.

"I knew they would get it. How exciting for them. I don't think it could have happened to a better group of people." She pauses for a second before continuing. "Speaking of, did you get a chance to talk to Phoenix?" I didn't tell her that I let him ass fuck me in the storage room Friday night. I simply told her that we had things to talk about, in regards to how he left the hotel that morning. That much I had told her about. As of late, I've been hiding a lot from her. I guess I just don't want to hear the negativity. I know that she looks out for me, but she fucks without attachment. Why can't it be the same for me? I won't tell her about the whole dominant/submissive aspect of our arrangement, but I have decided to tell her that we have an arrangement. A fuck one.

"Yeah. We've decided to keep seeing each other." She raises an eyebrow, and I quickly clarify. "Not like that. Neither of us wants a relationship, but we can admit that we want to fuck each other."

"This sounds more like him talking, and I haven't even talked with him much." She rolls her eyes in exasperation. "You're going to get your heart broken," she warns.

"Goddamn, Irelyn. This is why I didn't want to tell you. What's wrong if I just want some dick? You freaking do it all the time," I huff.

"Exactly. I do this all the time. I can separate the emotional from just having a good fuck," she retorts. "Up until a couple of months ago, you wouldn't even let a man get near your pussy. You don't have the same experience as me, and you're damn sure not on his level when it comes to "just fucking." He's already changing you, and you can't see it." I don't want to hear her confirm the same shit he said. I turn over in the bed, away from her. Thank God I didn't share the other shit.

"Whatever," I mumble. "You don't have to worry about it. I'm seeing him Wednesday, and I'm going to fuck his brains out." She laughs at this and pulls my shoulder until I'm looking at her.

"I think you have that one backward. You will be the one getting fucked." I try to turn back over, but she straddles me. "Don't be mad, Harlow. I will support your decision. If you want to play in the big leagues, then do it. I will be here to support you, no matter what." I stare up at her and see the sincerity in her eyes. What she is really saying is, she thinks I'm going to get hurt, but she'll be around to pick up the pieces. She doesn't have the whole picture, and her reaction is exactly why I can't tell her.

"I know. I'm a big girl, okay? I don't want you to keep seeing me as this fragile person you need to shelter. I don't want to be that girl anymore. Don't make me."

"Okay, babe. I'm here." She leans down and gives me the biggest hug. I'm still not going to tell her everything, but this is a start.

"Mm-hmm." She pulls the cover back and holds it tight to her chest. "Come on. Let's go get breakfast. We need a game plan for Wednesday."

"Oh, Jesus," I gripe.

"No, Oh, Jesus. We need you to be ready. You need a Brazilian wax, so your friend downstairs will be ready." So it seems my pussy has yet another name—comical. I'm not opposed, I guess.

"I don't want to make a big deal out of this."

"Too late," she sings. "You need sexier panties and bras, at least. Give him the package. Make it fun for him to unwrap. I think lingerie is kind of like its own form of foreplay—something to look forward to. After you're waxed to perfection, we need to get you some sexy black lace. It will look great against your skin."

"Irelyn," I chastise. She is already getting carried away. Who the hell does she think is going to pay for all of this?

"What? You want to play in the big leagues, right? You can't show up still wearing Hello Kitty on your panties. That's not hot. A bit pedophile, but not hot," she laughs. She needs to stay the hell out of my underwear drawer. I only have one pair of Hello Kitty panties. They're mostly what I call cotton full backs in my drawer. I call them that because they cover everything, but they're comfy.

I'm not completely out of touch with what it means to be sexy. I do own a couple of sexy pairs of lace panties. That is what I wore the last two times I hooked up with Phoenix. On second thought, it may be smart to purchase a few more. I don't want him to think those are the only two that I own, even though that is the case.

"We can go shopping Tuesday and do that Brazillian wax thing," I suggest.

"Waxing tomorrow and shopping on Tuesday. This will give you a chance to acclimate to the waxing and deal with any redness before you see Phoenix," she corrects. Gah, this already sounds like too much. I hope he appreciates all of this.

"Fine." I get up finally to search for something to put on. "Let's get breakfast, so I can probe your sex life now," I chide. If we talk about her, it will take the focus off me.

I don't want to work myself into a ball of nerves before the time even comes. I prefer to fantasize about what is to come when I'm alone. If that orgasm he brought me to last night, without even being here is any indication, I'm ready. A shy hot mess, but ready. I couldn't be any more of a contradiction of feelings right now. I want it, but I'm slightly nervous about the how and what of it all. I've seen a glimpse of a different Phoenix when he slips into control mode—I can't explain it. It's like it's him, but not. I let Irelyn's voice fade to the background as she starts talking again about her hook up last night.

CHAPTER TWENTY-ONE

Phoenix

I watch as she looks around the suite, trying desperately to hide her nerves. She mentions how nice it is, but it is the least of my focus. She's worn another fitted dress, which is so out of touch with who she is. I wouldn't care of she was wearing a potato sack, but we'll work on that. Right now, my dick strains against the tightness of my jeans. I watch her delectable ass nearly swallow the hemline of her dress. She has to tug on it every few seconds to keep it from riding up. I walk over and find the control panel embedded in the wall that generates the music. I press play, and Beyonce's "Haunted" fills the room. Sexy enough.

"Come here, Harlow," I ask firmly, but with finesse. I will need to ease her into my commands. She doesn't say a word. She comes to me and instinctually looks down. Her shyness shines through like a beacon. "Look at me." She looks up at me through her eyelashes, and her innocence to all of this tugs at my heart. I'm going to strip that all away. I'm a selfish bastard. I shouldn't want to taint her with my darkness, but it is beyond my control. I haven't wanted anything as much as I want this in a long time.

"Yes," she says simply as if she is answering so many unasked questions—extinguishing any doubts that remain. She is giving me the green light to proceed.

SHE LOOKS IN THE DIRECTION OF THE BEDROOM, AND I smile wickedly. How vanilla of her. She is about to get her first lesson. In a split second, I grab her and spin her until her back is to the wall behind us. My arms extend to the wall on each side of her head. "I want you to release my dick from my pants and stroke me." My voice is purposely a little more direct this time. I want to see how she responds. Baby steps. "No hesitation," I add.

"Okay," she whispers. She slowly unbuttons my jeans with trembling fingers. She reaches in and finds that I'm commando and hard as fuck already. She releases me, and my dick juts toward my navel. She takes me in her hand and strokes me as I have instructed. A bead of wetness forms on the tip of my dick. She doesn't stop her long, slow strokes. She just uses it to lubricate me well. I let her play until her hooded eyes give away her readiness. I grab the hemline of her dress and raise it above the curve of her ass.

"I didn't tell you to stop," I chastise when she pauses to see what I'm going to do next. I wait until she continues her strokes before I slip a finger into her black lace thong. It's quite sexy. Too bad it's a waste. I soak my finger in her juices as I add a second finger to glide through her wetness. "So slick," I observe.

MY FINGERING HAS HER SO DISTRACTED, BUT THAT'S kind of the point, though. I get a grip on the thin piece of fabric, and with one rip, it is snatched away from her body. Her eyes widen in surprise. She opens her mouth to protest, but I silence her with the same finger that was just wreaking havoc on her pussy.

"Shhhhhh, princess." I rub the wetness across her lips. "Open." She complies, and I insert my fingers into her mouth so she can see how good she tastes. Her eyes look upward in confusion and thought. I can tell that she is processing my commands and is still in her own head. That just won't do. I need her in subspace. She licks my fingers, one at a time, and it is so erotic. I use my other hand to keep fingering her until that telltale sign of her shaking legs lets me know that she is close to an orgasm. She is so fucking responsive. I can feel my dick hardening even more in her petite hands. She is barely stroking me now as her own impending orgasm rocks her body. I remove my fingers from her soaking pussy to give her the first lesson of edging—orgasm denial at it's finest.

"Phoeeeenix" she whines around my fingers. "Please." I smack her ass, but not enough to cause her pain—

simply to get her attention. I remove my fingers from her mouth and lift one of her legs to wrap around my hip.

SHE IMMEDIATELY INSERTS MY DICK WHERE SHE SO desperately needs me. I let her for now. I pacify her with a few generous strokes, but just short enough to prohibit the pinnacle she is trying to reach. Her ass wiggles as she tries to top, but I control the tempo with a simple angling of my hips against her. I gently caress her neck.

"Remember, you can say no at any time. You can tell me to stop." She nods her head to let me know that she remembers. "I want to try breath play with you."

"Breath what?" I explain that it is a form of choking, but the whole point is to deny her air for periods to enhance the orgasm. It can be scary, even when you know it's coming. I don't know how she will react to it. "Just let me show you. Stop me if it's too much. You can just tap my arm, and I will stop immediately. Okay?"

"Okay." She wiggles her ass again as she tries to pull me closer to her. My caress of her neck transitions to me, wrapping my hand around her neck, as I gradually increase the intensity of my strokes. I tighten my grip as she begins to fuck me back. I watch the initial shock fade from her face as I loosen my grip to allow her to breathe again. I set a varying tempo, slowly denying her breath as I pound into her. I know the moment she enters subspace.

. . .

She closes her eyes, and her entire body relaxes in my arms. It's so fucking beautiful. I have to be careful for the both of us—for her safety. I'm careful not to suppress her breath too long that she slips into unconsciousness. I only want her in a state of euphoria. Her life is literally in my hands, and the control empowers me. Addicting.

"Feel me, Harlow. Feel your life in my hands." With each thrust into her warm, inviting pussy, it gets harder to deny my own orgasm. Breath play is more enjoyable than I could have possibly imagined. I haven't done this to anyone else, besides Melissa—my last serious relationship. My balls slap against her ass as I drive into her. Her pussy clenches around me, and I'm right there with her. I apply pressure to her neck as we both ride out the best fucking nut ever. I release her neck, and she falls limp in my arms, completely spent.

"That was. That was." She can't even finish her sentence. She just clings to me. I know she needs what is formally called aftercare: basically, me to comfort her until she comes down from the high. I sweep her up in my arms and walk her to the bedroom. I had so much more planned for her, but it will have to wait a bit. I anticipated the possibility that she would drop this deep just because she hadn't experienced this level of pleasure before. It's a dump of endorphins by the body that causes a feeling similar to intoxication.

. . .

It would be unsafe to continue another scene with her since her decision-making ability to protest has been compromised. I lay her on the bed while I get her a glass of water. When I return, she is just lying there, curled up with a lazy grin on her face. I crawl up behind her and sit her up so she can take a few sips. After I'm satisfied that she is hydrated, I pull her in my arms and just hold her. I don't cuddle, but this is what she needs right now: to feel safe. Eventually, her heart rate slows, and her breathing evens out. Once she falls into a slumber, I feel comfortable enough to join her. I never let her go. Instead, I fall asleep with the woman who has given me the most beautiful gift—her submission.

Harlow

I awake to strong muscular arms wrapped around my waist. I'm disoriented for a second, but then I remember I am here with Phoenix. I'm not sure how much time has passed, but I know I've been fucked well. Some parts are a blur, but I remember being frightened and a suffocating sensation before an intense feeling of pleasure took over my body. It's indescribable other than I felt like I was floating. My pussy is delectably sore from the punishment she took, but it is the good kind of sore.

Phoenix is an enigma. I wouldn't have guessed he was capable of any of this, just to look at him.

I MEAN, WHO WOULD HAVE THOUGHT THAT THIS SEXY guy, who doesn't look like your typical rocker to begin with, had so many layers? To know that although he could be considered a manwhore, this is a side of himself that he keeps reserved. I got to see the part of him that he rarely shows to anyone. I'm feeling pretty damn special at the moment, as I bask in the afterglow of the start of something great.

"Hmm, you're awake," Phoenix says groggily. I can feel his muscular chest against my back. Oddly I'm naked, but he is still in his jeans. "How are you feeling?"

"More than great, I'd say." There is just enough sunlight shining through the crack in the blackout drapes that I can see him smiling with pride. "Why am I the only one naked, though?"

"It was for your benefit. You needed to be comfortable, but you also needed to rest after our breath play scene. Had I gotten naked with you, I can't say that I would not have rolled you over during the night and slid into you. Your pussy chips away at my self-control." All I heard through all that is I needed to rest.

"So we stopped because of me?" So much for handling the big leagues, as Irelyn would put it.

"No worries, Harlow. It was to be expected. I wouldn't

be worth my salt if I didn't anticipate your reaction, especially with it being your first time."

PHOENIX EXPLAINS TO ME WHAT SUBSPACE MEANS AND the importance of aftercare. It was important for him not to push because me being under the influence of heightened euphoria wouldn't be conducive to further play. I couldn't properly consent to the pleasure he wanted to inflict on my body.

"Well, we can continue now," I offer embarrassingly.

"Maybe. First, let's run you a bath." He gets up out of the bed and opens the curtains fully to let the natural sunlight in. The muscles in his back, coupled with his jeans sitting low on his hips, are hot as hell. His bare feet, though, are everything. I'm not really into feet, but there is just something about a man wearing nothing but jeans and exposed bare feet—kind of primal. It's sexy. I'm getting worked up just watching him move about the room. It's unfair for someone to be that hot and gorgeous without doing anything—just normal shit. I want to fuck him right now. He makes me crazy with lust, yet I can't just blurt it out what I want. He walks past me into the bathroom. Seconds later, I hear water running. I pull the covers back and decide to join him. First, I have to slip my dress on, which is lying on the floor. I'm not that confident to walk around naked. "You could have stayed in bed until your water was ready," he mentions.

"It's okay. I'm up now." The truth is, I feel a need to

be near him. His natural scent is intoxicating. I know I don't have long with him, as we'll be checking out of the hotel in a few hours. I want to make the most of our time.

"You can get in now," he says as he turns off the water.

"Uh, okay." He is different this morning. It's crazy, but I want domineering Phoenix back. He says, and I do. No time to be in my own head and create self-doubts. How do I tell him what I want? It's like my body knows how much I want the dick, but I'm afraid to speak the words. Fear of rejection paralyzes the words on my tongue. His maybe response in the bedroom to my hint at continuing where we left off doesn't do anything for my confidence. Hell, I don't even want to get nude in order to get in the tub while he is still standing here. The bright light of this bathroom negates any place to hide. He would see everything.

"You're doing it again, Harlow," he observes. Only I don't know what he is getting at.

"Doing what?" I know he is about to call me out on something.

"Overthinking. Hiding. You pick." He stares through me, and I can't keep his gaze. He has me pegged.

"I'm—" I'm about to deny his accusations, but he shushes me.

"Shhhh," he says, bringing a lone finger to his lips. I remember that same finger pressed against my lips after it had stroked me and soaked me. "I can see it your eyes.

Your face is very telling. It gives away what you're feeling." He stands up from the edge of the tub and walks over to me. He pulls down the dress I just put back on. He inches it down to expose my breasts first, perusing the hardening of my nipples.

"Let me help you," he offers. He pulls my dress the rest of the way down and lets it fall to my ankles. I'm completely naked, and I struggle not to cover myself with my hands. "Good girl," he praises. "Now undress me." *Holy shit.* His Dom voice is back. I unbutton his jeans and pull them down his legs until he steps out of them. He stands there proud with his dick at attention. It is pink perfection—so pretty.

"Gorgeous," I say, immediately realizing my inner thoughts have manifested into speech.

"Why, thank you. He likes you, too." He winks. He walks around me and steps in the tub. "Join me, Harlow." I step into the tub, and I'm guided to straddle him. He rubs himself against me, and I already feel I'm teetering on the edge. His cock is hard and waiting for me. I slide down on it to the hilt. I begin to rock on it. But my motions are halted.

"What's wrong?" I question.

"I say when, princess." My control freak is back...okay, maybe he never left. "What are the magic words?" he teases.

"Please, Sir," I say mockingly as I roll my eyes. What

does he want me to say? He's made me horny, and I want to fuck. I'm caught off guard by what happens next. He lifts me up off his dick and stands. He exits the tub quite pissed with me. His jaw tightens, and nostrils flare. *What the?* I don't understand.

CHAPTER TWENTY-TWO
Phoenix

I will not stand to be mocked. I don't give her an explanation. She needs to figure it out. This is not some pretend world I live in. I'm not exactly proud of my urges to control women by unconventional means —the need to bring them to the brink of suffocation or death as a way to exert my power. The feeling is unparalleled by anything else. I have other urges that are prominent in my kink repertoire, but breath play is definitely my strongest itch. Regardless of my desire for her, I will not allow Harlow to make light of what I've chosen to share with her. It's not for everyone, and I understand that. I would never push. However, if we're not in the same mindset or seriousness of what we partake in, I will end it. I saw the joke in her eyes. Last night, her submission was something to see—beautiful. Today, I'm at a loss. I see her attempts to pacify me, say what's needed to get what she wants. I will not allow this to be a game, and I damn sure will not allow her to top.

I walk over and turn the shower on. Let her bathe on her own, and then we're out of here. I'm done. I pretend not to notice as she steps out of the tub. Worry is all over her face. She can't hide shit. I can tell she realizes her mistake. The submissive in her doesn't like that she's made me upset.

She comes to the shower and stands on the outside for a second. Seeing her so unsure, but making the effort anyway, defuses my frustration. Maybe I am being too hard on her. I can't expect her to acclimate and adjust to my needs in a day. I will give her a chance to show me this is what she wants—that this is not just some sick joke to her. Harlow steps into the shower with me, and no words are exchanged. She drops to her knees, ready to deliver her apologies directly to my cock. She is forgiven with the first timid lick, but I'm inclined to let her show me just how sorry she is.

"Good girl," I praise to encourage her. This rebuilds her confidence. She strokes me with one hand as she gives her undivided attention to the head. Her warm tongue licks the vein that runs underneath my dick, and it makes my toes curl. "Shit, baby."

"Mm-hmm," she moans around my dick. The vibrations have me putting my hand against the travertine for support. She takes me deep, and I love that her gag reflex is almost nonexistent. She bobs up and down in slow, excruciatingly pleasurable licks. I feel the buildup at the base of my balls, but I can't come yet. I need to fuck her. In an instant, I take my dick out of her mouth and pull her up. I push her against the shower wall. "Grrrrrr. Fucking hold on."

I SLIDE INTO HER AND IMMEDIATELY BEGIN TO THRUST into her roughly. My control has snapped. I wrap my hands around her hair and pull as I slam into her over and over. She pushes her ass out toward me for more, and it ignites my frenzied pace. My balls slapping against her ass echoes over the sound of the shower. I'm not going to last. Her pussy is too good, and I've denied myself this too long. Rough sex is my other kink, but I wanted to build up to it. Too late. I use my other hand to finger her. I need her to catch up. The slickness that coats my fingers tells me that she is already there. I bite her shoulder as the most intense orgasm rips through me. She clenches around my dick, prolonging it even more. It's not until I've totally emptied myself into her that I realize my mistake. "Fuccccccccck," I groan and not in a pleasant tone. She can tell. Her own realizations are apparent.

"Condom. You didn't wear a condom." She is having her own mini breakdown. I slide out of her, and some of my cum drips down her leg. "I don't have unprotected sex." The worry is back—etched deep within crinkles in her forehead.

"Relax. This is a fucking first for me too. I'm not going to give you anything. Are you on the pill?" The harshness in my tone has bite. It's not her fault. It's mine.

I'M UPSET BECAUSE I PRIDE MYSELF ON NOT ONLY THE control I exert but being in control. I've already taken so many liberties with her—relaxed my rules. And now this.

"No," she answers. There is more to consider than just an STD here. She opens one of the soaps in the shower enclave and begins to scrub herself furiously.

"Dammit." I knew the answer to that question before I asked it. I'm quite sure she wasn't getting dick regularly before she met me if her earlier clothing choice was anything to go by. "I don't fuck around without protection, Harlow. So that is one less thing to worry about. Finish your shower, and we'll see about getting you that Plan B thing on the way back," I say more calmly. I step in next to her and use the soap she just set down to wash my dick. Good enough. I get out and towel myself dry. Although there were highlights, I wouldn't call our attempt at this a success.

I feel myself changing for her, and I don't like it. She gets underneath my skin like no other. I give her consideration that nobody else gets—I bend the rules for her. The last woman who was able to get this close to me broke me. Melissa introduced me to all of this. She was an experienced sub who knew what she wanted. She saw dominant traits in me and got me into shit I didn't know existed or that I would grow to love.

Melissa gave me an outlet for my need for control, and then she left me. She made me love her, and then she walked away when she grew bored. I wasn't hardcore enough for her. She wanted more than I could give or wanted to experiment with. After she left, I hated this side of myself: the demons that needed this type of sex for true gratification. I'm able to suppress my urges for the most part, mainly because I don't find many women worthy of the effort. This lifestyle is not something you can venture into casually or lightly. Most women I meet are only my fuck for the night or, at best, three times. Not enough time to establish a real connection for what I need. There have been some that I have shared the lightest of my kink with just to subdue pent-up urges, but nothing like what I shared with Harlow last night or just now.

I lost control with her. She didn't seem to mind the rough sex, but it still doesn't sit right with me. I can barely look at her. To make matters worse, I lost my temper. I can't let her be another Melissa. I need to gain some perspective and regain control, or I will have to distance myself from her. For now, though, I have to fix this. I can't let her leave here thinking she did something wrong or that I'm angry with her.

. . .

"Look, Harlow. I'm sorry. I'm upset with myself, not you. I lost control." I leave it at that. I won't tell her about Melissa or why my need for control is so important.

"It will be fine. We'll get the Plan B. You say you haven't had unprotected sex, and neither have I, so we should be safe. Don't beat yourself up about it. If it's of any consequence, I'm not mad."

"Good. I don't want us to part on a sour note. I appreciate last night—your trust and submission. It's been a long time since I've indulged." I chuckle because that sounded like some goddamn admission in an anonymous meeting or something.

"What's funny?" she asks as she turns the shower off. I hand her a towel. It doesn't escape my notice that she is just a little more comfortable with her nudity than when we first came in here. She grabs the towel and wraps it around herself before stepping out of the shower. Okay, so maybe not totally comfortable. Baby steps.

"Never mind. I'll leave you to it, so we can check out." I smile. I'm still quite pissed with myself, but the responsible thing to do is not to let her see. Not after what she has given. I smile so her submissive nature can relax. I bring her small overnight bag into the bathroom so she can change. I leave out to give her the privacy she won't ask for. As I change in the bedroom, I look around the room. This is our second visit to this hotel. I question whether there will be another.

CHAPTER TWENTY-THREE

Harlow

It's a beautiful Sunday afternoon, and I'm heading to the lake house to see Asher. That's the cover story anyway. I really want to see Phoenix. Irelyn's mother delivered her Honda Accord to her and took a flight back earlier this week. She has been gracious enough to let me use it. I kept the details minimal about my night with Phoenix, and she didn't push. She did raise her eyebrow when I said I wanted to go see Asher. I'm not fooling her. She declined to come along. She said Mike was picking her up for a real date. Good for her. He must have been more impressive than she let on. It seems we both might be hiding a few things.

Honestly, I just need to reestablish my connection with Phoenix. He called on Thursday to see how I was doing, but that was it. I know he went down to Atlanta to celebrate their new record deal. I'd be lying if I say I wasn't just the tad bit jealous. Did he fuck somebody else this weekend? He said he wouldn't. That our arrangement was exclusive, but at this point, do we still have an arrangement? I don't want to come off as clingy, but I need reassurance that nothing has changed. I need to feel him out. How will he act when he sees me? I guess I'm going to find out because I'm pulling into the driveway now.

"Harlow? How did you get here?" Asher says when I walk into the living room. Shock registers on Phoenix's face as he turns to look at me from the couch. He has his feet propped up, looking at football.

"Irelyn has her car now, so I drove," I reply. "Sorry. The door was unlocked, so I let myself in."

"Oh, hush. This is your second home. I do wish you would have called, though," he says. "Lily is in town for a week. I was heading to pick her up from the airport, and we were going grab a bite before I brought her back here to meet the guys. Well, they're out right now except for Phoenix. You can come with me if you want. I do want you to meet her."

"No worries. Don't change your plans. I'm not going to be a third wheel. You guys need the alone time. I'll be here when you get back. I want to meet her too," I assure him.

"Are you sure?" He looks doubtful.

"Yes. This is my second home, remember? Go. I'll be here."

"Well, in that case, see you in a few hours." He hugs me and waves bye to Phoenix, who hasn't said a word. Once Asher is out the door, I go over and sit next to him.

"Hi," I say as I smile at him. He looks over at me and smiles back.

"Hello, Harlow." He grabs the remote next to him and starts to scroll through the guide. "I guess it's just you and me, huh?"

"I GUESS SO." I WATCH AS HE STOPS ON A RECORDING OF *Elementary*. "You didn't have to turn off your football."

"Meh. It's just something to watch. My Cowboys aren't playing today, so it's no big deal."

"Well, okay then." It has been a while since I had a chance to just veg out and watch my shows.

"Have you seen this episode?" he asks as he highlights the oldest recording.

"No. Looks like I've missed a lot." I laugh.

"Well, we do have the afternoon." He grins. He lies down and stretches out on the sofa. He pats a spot next to him that he has made. I don't know how to react. He wants me to lay with him. This is yet another layer of Phoenix. This is not my "let's fuck and have an arrangement" guy. Unless this is leading to that—like "*Elementary* and Chill" coined from "Netflix and Chill." I laugh.

"What's funny, woman? Get over here." He motions again for me to join him. I'll play along. I lie down next to him, and he pulls me closer into his arms. I melt into him, but something is off. I can't put my finger on it. Maybe I'm just pessimistic, but his explanation of the type of relationship we would have left no room for doubt. He was clear, and this is not it. Maybe since we've shared our first scene, as he called it, he has had a change of heart, and this is the only way he knows to show it.

IT FEELS GOOD TO BE CUDDLED IN HIS ARMS, TO FEEL wanted. I didn't expect to feel this way. I can admit that I'm starting to let him into my heart, and that frightens the shit out of me. Nobody has gotten this far with me. I know his reputation and the fame that is coming his way, yet my heart wants him. *When the fuck did that happen?* I can't share these feelings with him, though. No, I think he'd run. Hopefully, this is an indication that he is starting to have feelings for me too. I just have to let him process it his own way and be at peace with it. I snuggle into him more, dizzy on his scent. He is wearing some cologne that is so hypnotic. This is new.

"How was the celebration with the label?" He pulls me closer and kisses me on the forehead. What the hell is he trying to do to me? His Dom side gets me worked up, but this new expression of tenderness is really getting to me.

"It was—" I cut him off with my lips on his. He pauses at first in surprise before he kisses me back. And oh man, does he kiss me back. He flips me so that I'm now lying on top of him, and he can palm my ass. Even though I'm wearing my usual jeans and T-shirt, I can feel the hardness of his cock through his gym shorts.

Harlow

PHOENIX DEEPENS THE KISS, AND I RUB MYSELF AGAINST his hardness—so desperate for the Dom to take over, so he can give me what he knows I want. He's not making an appearance, so I force myself to be brave,

"Fuck me, Phoenix. Please, Sir." He stops kissing me and sits up. His brows creases. I'm afraid that I've done something wrong again. I try to hold on, but he moves my hands. Maybe he felt like I was making a mockery of our D/s relationship again. Shit, I don't know, but whatever I said or did, it's like I doused him with a bucket of cold water.

"Look. Umm. I have to go. Sorry, Harlow."

"Don't run. Don't you dare fucking run! You tell me right now what I did, or this is fucking over. Do you hear me? I can't keep doing your hot and cold bullshit." My feelings are hurt. He gave me a sample of something special, and now he is yanking it from under me.

"You didn't do anything okay. Just please give me some time. Nothing's changed. I promise. Don't be upset. I have to leave for a bit, but I'll be back. We're okay. I'm not running. I just need some time to figure some things out." He says all of that in a rush. He is running, but he has asked me to be patient in a roundabout way. I knew all of this was out of character for him, so I give him the time he needs to process his feelings.

It's okay to be scared. I think we're unintentionally changing each other—changing our views on what we thought we wanted. I won't be that girl: the one who has to have all the answers right now. I will give him the time he needs, within reason.

"Okay. We'll talk later."

"Sure." He plants a quick kiss on my forehead, and then he is gone. I don't know what is happening between us, but one thing is for sure; it is more than either of us bargained for or planned. I lie on the sofa and continue watching *Elementary* in a haze. I don't even know when I drifted off to sleep.

~

"Harlow. Wake up. I want you to meet Lily," Asher says, shaking me. It takes me a moment to orient myself. I rub the sleep from my eyes to find a raven-haired beauty with the prettiest green eyes I've ever seen staring down at me. I sit up to completely take her in. She's gorgeous.

"Hello," I say, extending my hand to her. "Nice to meet you. My brother has told me so much about you."

"All good things, I hope." She smiles, and she has dimples. She is just too perfect. She's wearing a simple sundress and has a cute bob haircut. I'm getting good vibes from her and a sense of genuineness.

"Yes. All good things. How was your flight?" Lily tells me about her layovers and how excited she is to finally get here. Irelyn has to meet her. She is just too adorable. Great first impression.

I'M HAPPY FOR ASHER. KIND OF JEALOUS AT THE SAME time, I guess. He gets to have a normal relationship—one he doesn't have to hide.

"Oh, is that *Elementary*?" she asks excitedly. "I love that show." Yup, definitely a keeper.

"Yeah, me, too. I think in the end it was watching me, though," I joke.

"I would say so. You were knocked out when we came in," Asher agrees.

"Well, the house got a little quiet with everyone gone," I say. I got bored.

"Uh, no. Phoenix is here. His bike is parked out front. He must be upstairs in his room." Asher looks toward the stairs. "He has taken the room back that you were using."

"I would think so. It was his room first," I say in a matter-of-fact manner. I wonder if he is actually here. If he is, I can't believe he came back and didn't tell me. Is he avoiding me?

"It's dark out now, but I still want to show Lily the deck and the lake. The path is lit, so it'll be nice. We'll be right back in," Asher announces, successfully interrupting my thoughts.

"Okay. You two go ahead." Asher grabs her hand and leads her out the door. They're barely out the door before I take the stairs, two at a time. I need to know if Phoenix is really here. When I reach the top of the stairs, the arguing on the other side of the cracked bedroom door confirms that he is.

"What the fuck, Sevyn?" he questions. Who is Sevyn? At first, I think someone is in the room with him until I see him pass the door with his cell phone attached to his ear. Unfortunately, he sees me too, so I've been busted trying to eavesdrop. That wasn't my original intent, but I'm sure that is not the way it looks. "I'll have to call you back." He hangs up the phone and then comes to the doors and opens it wider.

"You can come in, Harlow," he says as he gestures for me to come in.

"I didn't mean to interrupt your conversation. I promise I wasn't eavesdropping," I explain.

"Okay. Are you going to come in?" I continue standing in the doorway for a few seconds before I finally accept his invite.

"How long have you been back? Why didn't you wake me?" I fire in rapid succession. I know Asher may not be outside long, and I don't want to be caught up here when he gets back.

"You looked like you were really tired, so I didn't want to disturb you," he says by way of explanation. I'm about to see if he is ready to talk about earlier, but then his phone rings in his hand. He looks down to see who's calling before answering.

"Hello, Desiree. How's it going?" His face brightens and puts a finger up as a motion to hold that thought. He walks away toward the bedroom window to continue their conversation.

"I KNOW THAT SUCKS. TELL YOU WHAT. WHY DON'T you have dinner with us? I was just getting ready to throw something together. I'm sure Asher would have no problem picking you up." So it's Desiree. I don't know why, but that woman rubs me the wrong way for some reason. "The guys aren't here, but they should be back any minute. And don't worry, it's no problem at all." From his one-sided conversation, I gather Desiree is coming here. He says he will see her soon and ends the call.

"Sorry. That was Desiree," Phoenix says. As if I hadn't figured that part out. "She was heading to Los Angeles from here, but her flight has been delayed until morning. It would be ludicrous for her stay at the airport all that time."

"Hotel, maybe?" I say under my breath.

"Huh?"

"Nothing. Well, I better get back downstairs, so Asher

isn't looking for me." I hate that I'm feeling jealous. Shit is getting so blurred.

"Oh, okay. I guess since the guys aren't here, I should be the one to pick her up from the airport. Asher is with his girl, so I'll go." I cringe. Asher is with his girl as if he isn't. I'm not his girl. The fact that this bothers me signifies that my feelings are starting to change. I'm terrified. Worse yet, I can't tell him for fear that he doesn't feel the same. It could ruin everything.

"I'm going to go." I turn and hurry back downstairs. There is no sign of Asher and Lily.

A FEW MINUTES LATER, PHOENIX PASSES THE LIVING room on his way out the door. "Tell Asher I'm taking the truck to go get Desiree. I'll bring dinner back since I can't do both."

"Sure," I reply without taking my eyes off the TV. I don't even know what show this is. When Asher comes in with Lily, I fill him in.

"I think I may head back," I mention casually. The truth is, I'm in a jealous, pissy mood. I've just come to the realization that I want Phoenix as more than just a friend —more than an arrangement.

"You have to stay," Asher pleads. "I want you to get to know Lily. We've already eaten, but we can have a few bites of whatever Phoenix brings back."

"I didn't want to intrude on your time, but if you're

sure, I'll stick around for a bit," I lie to cover up my hesitancy.

"We're sure," Lily speaks up. We sit around the dinner table, and we talk about school and majors. She's an education major and has considered transferring to the University of Alabama to be closer to Asher. Now that he is going on the road soon to tour, they've even considered her taking online classes, so the flexibility would leave her free to travel. They are just so happy together. The sacrifices they are willing to make for each other are evident. I want a piece of that. Someone who's willing to make me a part of their plans and isn't afraid to commit to making a real relationship work.

~

I PICK AT MY CHINESE FOOD AS THE GUYS DISCUSS THEIR upcoming tour in a few months. My stomach is already sour because I know my time with Phoenix will come to an end.

"I've negotiated for you guys to have a slightly bigger tour bus than originally planned. It has one master bedroom and four bunks, but the space is luxurious and ample. You guys deserve to travel in style," Desiree shares.

"Is it costing us more money from our advancement?" Phoenix asks.

"Nope. The company we use for our other bands agreed to give me a deal in exchange for exclusivity." She smiles.

"Well, in that case, I'm ecstatic." Phoenix winks. She touches his arm as she laughs, and I want to puke. They are openly flirting with each other. "As our business manager, are you going to be traveling with us?" I want to wipe that stupid grin right off his face. Hello? I'm sitting right here, asshole. Couldn't you wait until I wasn't around to try to get in her pants?

"Not all the time, but I will be with you guys some, especially in the beginning to orient you all to how things work. You all aren't going to want me around once you start having groupies wanting to follow you," she teases. What an insensitive bitch. She sees that Asher's girl is sitting there, and she has no qualms about painting the pictures of whores on the bus with them.

"Oh, you don't have to worry about that. We don't allow those women into our personal space. We don't do it here at the house and wouldn't do it on the road."

I push my plate of food away. Killian and Ren nod in agreement, while Asher and Lily seem to be engaged in their own private conversations. I tap my fingers on the table, contemplating an excuse to leave. I didn't miss Phoenix's future tense prediction in that statement. He is planning to have groupies, just not on the bus. I knew our arrangement would be short-lived, but it just feels like a slap in the face to hear him say it.

"If you say so. The road and fame change people," Desiree continues.

"Well, I have my girl right here," Asher finally speaks up. He leans over and kisses Lily on the cheek, and she blushes. Good for him. I knew I didn't like this witch. She's rude, and she's been eye-fucking Phoenix since she got here. I can't do it. My blood is boiling. I need to go. I have no ties to Phoenix, and he has obviously already entertained thoughts of what it's going to be like on tour, even though he was just in my pussy a few days ago. I'm sure he and Desiree will end up fucking too. I can see the pull between those two. His consideration for her staying alone at the airport and wondering if she will be on the bus with them are the first two clues.

I take my plate to the kitchen and scrape the uneaten food in the trash. "I'm going to go, Asher. Nice meeting you, Lily." I won't even look at Phoenix.

"Drive safe, sis. Give me a call when you make it back." Lily waves goodbye, and I force a smile and wave back. I grab my purse and blink away the tears as I head to the car. I get in and fumble with finding the key. I wish she had the push start one. When I finally find the key and put it into the ignition, I look up to see Phoenix standing in front of the car. The beams of light reflect on him as he crosses those muscular arms of his. He comes around and knocks on the window. I lower it just enough to hear what he is saying.

"What's wrong, Harlow?"

"Nothing. Go back to your company." I try to raise the

window, but he slams his hand down on the top of the glass.

"Open the damn door, Harlow," he growls. "Company? She's our fucking manager. I knew you were jealous. Question is why?"

"I'm not jealous, asshole. Now move your fucking hand before it gets smashed," I retort.

"Lies. You can't hide shit. I read your face in there. It tells on you every time." I reverse the car, just a little, to encourage him to let go, and he uses his other hand to slap the top of the car.

"Stop! Goddamnit, stop! I swear I will fucking cause a scene. You want Asher to find out about us tonight?" That gets my attention.

"You wouldn't." Asher would flip his shit. This could mess up everything for them. The band needs to be cohesive to succeed.

They can't afford any conflict among them while they're trying to establish themselves. What would be the point of telling Asher? Our relationship isn't going anywhere. Hell, we don't even have a relationship. We have an arrangement, or at least we had. Right now, I'm not so sure.

"I would. Now put the car in park and open the door." He has me, and he knows it. He has to know that our exposure would be bad for the band, so why would he threaten that? I close my eyes in defeat, for a moment, before I do as he says. As soon as I open the door, he grabs my hand and pulls me out of the car. He spins me around, and my back is against the passenger window. "What's going on with you? You have no reason to be jealous. This is why I don't do relationships," he huffs.

"You do what you want. I don't care. What is the point of all this?" I say, gesturing around us. Why make this huge deal over what he presumes I'm feeling?

"I like what we started, and I don't want it to end. I promised you exclusivity, and that is what I will give."

"Are you sure, Phoenix? Because all you've been doing is running. You freaked the fuck out Thursday morning about losing control with me, and then again this afternoon when I asked you to fuck me. So you tell me what's going on." Phoenix backs away from me and runs both hands through his hair. He paces back and forth in front of me, obviously frustrated.

CHAPTER TWENTY-FOUR

Phoenix

Harlow just called me out on my shit, and I know she's right. I've been all over the map with her. As of Thursday, I didn't even know if I wanted to continue my arrangement with her. I don't like that she can make me lose control or bend my rules. Yet I'm drawn to her like a magnet. She has resurrected another one of my flaws tonight, which is associated with my unquantifiable need for control. I didn't mean for it to happen. It has already played out, and she has no idea. *Jealousy*. I purposely inflict it. It is a subset of my control. I wasn't completely honest with Harlow. True, I don't spank as a form of punishment, but my alternatives can be so much worse. The thing is, I never said there wouldn't be any punishment. I use jealousy as a means to make one feel how I want them to feel. I guess, in a sense, it is pain —emotional pain.

The significance is that I've only ever done this to

Melissa. It's probably another reason it was so easy for her to walk away from me in the end. It's another reason I can't have a normal relationship, even if I desire one. The minute I would feel her pulling away from me or feel like I was losing my ability to control her, I would make her jealous of another woman. Her emotional torment was her punishment and the gratification of power exchange for me. Her dependence on my love reassured me she wouldn't leave me. Only she eventually did.

I THOUGHT I WAS OVER THE NEED TO EXERT THIS because it has been a couple of years since I've done it. After Melissa, nobody else was worth this kind of effort. I had my rules, and I stuck to them until Harlow. The realization that she is under my skin, more than I thought, is a mind fuck. I should completely leave her alone. The fact that I've purposely tried to hurt her tonight because I felt her pulling away is a fucking overwhelming indicator that I have feelings for her. My ability to succeed at making her jealous tells me she has feelings for me too. We have obliterated the lines to this arrangement. I'm fucking selfish, though. I can't let her go.

"You're right," I finally tell her. "I lost control with you, and that really bothered me. I haven't been myself. I have personal stuff on my mind, but I do want to continue our arrangement."

"I don't know, Phoenix. This hot and cold is—" I don't let her finish that sentence. I'm on her in an instant. My mouth finds hers, and I coax her to open for me. She melts in my arms, and I know that I have her. She wraps her arms around my neck as I deepen the kiss. She's mine, and this kiss confirms it.

"Umm hmm." Desiree clears her throat behind us. *Shit. Busted.* "Does Asher know that you're out here sucking face with his sister?"

"That is none of your business," Harlow fires before I can get a word out.

"OH, TO THE CONTRARY, DEAR. I'M GUESSING ASHER doesn't know that the two of you are fucking, and that can destroy the chemistry of the band. So you see, it is my business." The two women stare each other down. I think I recognize jealousy in Desiree too, but that can't be. I've never touched her or given any indication that I wanted to. Yes, I've flirted a bit, but no more than I casually do with women as a persona.

"It's not what you think." Harlow looks like she wants to kick me in the balls with that statement. It's not like I can admit that Desiree's right. She wants to keep this quiet, just like I do. That is the only reason she opened the car door for me.

"Don't start lying to me, Phoenix. I'm pretty perceptive. I picked up on you two the day I came, and she was here. I'm surprised that Asher hasn't picked up on it or the other guys. Maybe she just hides it well, until you're around another woman. If those daggers she has been throwing me tonight is any indication, I'd say you've tapped that." She breaks her stare with Harlow to look at me. "And of course, it was your excuse to leave then, to make sure she didn't leave mad about your flirting with me tonight," she smirks.

"Okay, yes." Lying is useless at this point, so I just need to make sure she will keep her mouth closed. "Harlow and I are involved. It's private, so we'll just leave it at that. I trust that you will keep this to yourself." Harlow makes a move to get in the car, but I stop her. No way in hell is she leaving upset after we have gotten past the other shit.

"My lips are sealed, but be careful, darlings. This will blow up in your faces, but it's not my place to say anything. Just don't fuck up the morale of the band."

Our discussion is cut short by the Asher and Lily coming outside. I quickly step away from Harlow.

"Remember what I said," I whisper. "I want this with you." No explanation needed. She knows what "this" is.

. . .

"I was wondering where you all disappeared to," Asher says.

"We were seeing Harlow off," Desiree fills in quickly. "And I wanted to invite Harlow to lunch when I get back from Cali in a week." Harlow's face pales at this suggestion. I'm sure she'd rather cut an extremity off.

"Oh, that would be nice." Asher has no idea.

"Yes, I think so. I'm sure she will be around quite a bit, and it would be nice to get away from the testosterone from time to time. What do you say, Harlow?"

"Sure. Asher has my number. Call me when you get back." That fake smile on her face is almost believable. "Well, guys, I really do need to get on the road before it gets too late." She hugs her brother and mouths, "Later" to me.

At least there will be a later. Shit is getting more and more muddled with each passing day.

Harlow

I officially hate that Desiree bitch. Her conniving ways are glaringly obvious—so manipulative. She wants Phoenix, and I can see it. "You're not the only one that is perceptive," was what I wanted to say. I bit my tongue because I didn't want to make waves with their manager, but damn I wanted to slap her. Then she had the audacity to invite me to lunch—fake ass bitch. Gah, I'm fuming. I don't know what pisses me off more; the fact that I know that she is into Phoenix or that she tried to get in our business? I don't even want to think about her on the road with them. She looks like a woman who is used to getting what she wants.

Then there's Phoenix. He insists that he still wants our arrangement. That kiss was very convincing, so different from the one this afternoon. I think we're both struggling to make sense of what we're actually doing. The arrangement is okay, but I think it is a guise for what we are both feeling. I felt it in the way he held me this afternoon. I think it scared the shit out of him. This is new for me, too. I won't push, though. As long as we are moving forward, I will try to be patient. Progress is progress. I'm done lying to myself. I want more. What "more" is remains to be seen, though. I don't know what it looks like. I just know that I want whatever it is with him.

My cell rings, and I see that it is Phoenix calling. I can't talk to him right now. We will talk, but not now, while I'm so confused about what I want to say—how much I want to admit. I'm afraid all of this will end when I tell him the truth. He's going to run. I'm not trying to force him into anything, but I think it's important he knows where I stand. I will call him tomorrow. For now, I don't want to think about it.

I look over at Irelyn's bed and the ton of shit she has back on it. I'm guessing she is still out with Mike, but just in case she comes back, she needs to get in her own bed. I don't want any company tonight. I just want my space. I get like this when I'm sad. I'm sad because I'm worried about how tomorrow will play out once I confess to Phoenix that I have developed feelings. I walk over to Irelyn's bed and shove all her shit onto the floor until nothing is left. A little extreme? Maybe. I climb into my bed after changing into gym shorts and a tee. I just want to sleep so I don't have to think about anything. My phone rings a few more times before I turn the ringer off. *Sorry, Phoenix.* I cover my head with my blanket and wait for sleep to take me.

I FEEL ARMS WRAP AROUND MY WAIST. I'M READY TO ask Irelyn what the hell she is doing, but even in complete darkness, I can tell these are not Irelyn's arms. "Phoenix?"

"Shhhh. Yes, princess. Sleep." I have to be dreaming. How in the hell would he have gotten in here? He pulls me closer into his embrace, and I'm happy to indulge in the illusion. I close my eyes and let sleep take me under once again.

. . .

"Wake up, Harlow." I wake to Phoenix shaking me, and Irelyn standing over us with her arms crossed.

"He is going to get us in trouble if they find him up here," Irelyn says. I look up at him, and his messy bedhead makes me smile.

"Wait. How did you get in here?" I ask, finally snapping out of dreamland.

"I thought you snuck him in last night. I went to go sleep in Caroline's room," Irelyn says.

"Some blonde chick let me in last night. I think she said her name was Caroline. She felt sorry for me just sitting on the front steps outside."

"And why were you sitting outside? Didn't Harlow know you were out there?"

"She wouldn't answer her phone, so I had to drive an hour to see her. Then she didn't answer the phone for me to tell her I was here," Phoenix confesses. God. He has just opened a shit ton of worms for me. Irelyn is going to want to get to the bottom of this. She is like a dog with a bone.

At least it was Caroline. She is such a sweetheart. She won't tell anyone he's up here, but we now need a way to sneak him downstairs.

"I don't know what's going on between you two, but he needs to go now—before everybody wakes up. It's just after six now, so maybe we can get him out unseen." Phoenix jumps out of bed and starts to put on his shoes.

"Meet me outside in ten," he says before kissing me on the cheek. I smile like a giddy schoolgirl.

"Ah, hell," Irelyn groans as soon as he is out the door. "You have gone and caught feelings." My grin widens even more. "Stop grinning like a Cheshire cat. I knew you weren't ready for the big leagues. It's 'just fucking' she said. 'Just fucking' my ass. You're in love with him."

"Oh shut it, Irelyn. Let me have this moment. He came to be with me last night." Desiree was staying at the lake house until this morning, and he came to be with me. Maybe my little confession won't be so bad, after all. It gives me a little more confidence to tell him. I won't go as far as to say it's love, but I definitely feel strongly for him.

"The dick must have been really good to have you singing a different tune so quickly." She doesn't know the half of it because I haven't told her everything. This was a gradual build over a few months. I'm just finally at a point where I cannot only recognize it. I can admit it.

"God, I thought I was a pessimist." I shake my head as I pull a change of clothes out of my drawer. I need to shower, so it's going to be more than ten minutes.

"Just looking out for you, but I will say no more. I know that is not what you want to hear, so I'll stop. We do need to find some time to talk, though. I feel like I don't know what's going on with you anymore. We haven't had much time together lately."

"I agree. Let's talk later today." I plan on skipping my

history class this morning. I won't miss much. Besides, I have perfect attendance up until this point. I'll get the notes from Caroline.

"Fine. Don't forget." That pacifies her for now. I hurry down to our community bath so I can meet Phoenix.

∽

"What time is your class?" Phoenix asks as soon as I walk up to him. He is sitting on his motorcycle.

"Eight, but I'm not going."

"Uh. Yes, you are. I won't be the reason you miss class. We have an hour to talk and get breakfast before I head back." I fold my arms and pout, but he laughs. "That won't work on me, princess."

"Fine. Where are we going?"

"It's your campus. You tell me," he points out.

"I don't want to eat here. We don't have to go anywhere special, just away from here." I don't know how he is going to react. I'd rather not run into anyone I know in case the talk doesn't go as I would like it to.

"Okay. Cracker Barrel it is, then." He winks.

"Fine by me." I hop on the back of his bike, and it purrs to life. I hold on tight through the turns. I bury my nose into his shirt, committing his natural scent to memory, in case this is the last time. This morning will be our defining moment. Things can go either way, but I won't let him run. He will have to acknowledge my feelings and decide how we will proceed; none of this "we'll talk later" business. When we arrive, we get a quiet booth in the corner. We wait until the server takes our order before we address "the talk."

"We need to talk," we both blurt out at the same time. He laughs, and I join in, more so to hide my nerves.

"You first, princess," he says. Now I'm even more afraid. The little confidence I had going into this is gone. What if last night was meant to be a courtesy "let's go our separate ways" night? I mean, he didn't he try to have sex with me, and he refused to let me miss class this morning. He is heading back home after this. *Shit.* What if this is my final dismissal? "Get out of your head, Harlow. Just tell me what's on your mind. You're overthinking something, so just tell me."

I'm scared shitless, so I just blurt it out before I talk myself out of it. "I have feelings for you." He is too quiet. He just looks at me, and I don't know what to make of it. "Please say something."

CHAPTER TWENTY-FIVE
Phoenix

"Harlow. I already know." She bites her lip nervously, and I have to say it's quite endearing. I've been struggling with how to proceed from the moment I was able to admit to myself that I felt something for her too. I don't even want to think of her walking away. She has gotten further with me than anyone has in a long time, yet I know that she will walk out of my life if I can't give her what she is seeking. "I know because I feel it, too," I finally admit. The megawatt smile that forms on her lips is priceless. She lets out a sigh of relief. I'm sure that was hard for her to tell me.

"I'm glad to hear that. I didn't want to freak you out."

"I can't promise you anything. I will fuck up. I just ask for your patience."

"What are you saying, Phoenix?" I know that I have to try, or I will lose her. I will give her the relationship she wants.

"We can make it official," I finally say. "I want you to be mine. I already promised to be exclusive. Just don't expect me to be some over-the-top romantic douche because I'm not that guy." She grabs my hand across the table and squeezes.

"I don't want that guy. I want you. My Dom." Now I really wish I didn't have to do the responsible thing and let her go to class. I want to celebrate our new relationship while balls deep in her wetness.

OUR OMELETS ARRIVE, AND WE BOTH DIG IN. "SO WHEN do you want to tell Asher?" Harlow's face pales, and her fork clatters against her plate.

"I'm not sure if that is a good idea, right now. He is so protective of me. I don't want to cause tension for the band. Besides, you heard what Desiree said."

"Fine. We'll wait for now. I guess I need to show him I can abstain from the groupies first since I know that will be his biggest concern. We will have to eventually tell him, though. If he finds out on his own, he will be so pissed." She nods in agreement.

"We will. I think it needs to come from me." She pauses briefly before she continues. "What happens when you guys leave for your tour? What will happen with us?"

"Come with us." The minute that suggestion leaves my mouth, I wonder if that would be a good idea. Regardless, I'm willing to try.

"How? I have school."

"Well, I think Asher is trying to convince Lily to take online classes so that she could join us on the road sometimes. You could do the same thing. Couldn't you?" She wouldn't have to leave her life and friends to be on the road with us full-time, but taking online classes will give her flexibility for a visit.

"I'll have to see. I don't know if all the classes that I plan to take in the spring have an online option."

She takes a few bites of her omelet before she pushes it away. "I hope they do. I admit that it'll be nice. If I'm going to be a music journalist, it will be nice to see the whole picture."

"That's it? That's the only reason you would come?" I put my hand across my heart. "I'm crushed," I joke.

"Okay. Maybe it would be great to see you, too."

"Just maybe."

"Hush. Come on. I need to get to class if I'm going." I'm tempted to say fuck it and keep her to myself today, but I need to work on the selfish thing. I wave down our server to pay the bill.

"I can't let you be a slacker because of me." We're heading out the door, and I smack her ass. I love the roundness of it in the jeans she's wearing. She turns to look at me and gasps. She looks around to see if anyone saw that. Her face is so red right now.

"What? You're mine now, so everyone else can just fuck off. Your ass just looks too good in those jeans. Your fault." She slaps my shoulder and rushes to my bike. Yeah, this is going to be so much fun. She's about to find out what it really means to be mine. The gloves are really off now. I won't hold back. I hope she is strong enough to handle all of my demons because I plan to introduce her to each and every one of them. I just hope she doesn't run.

∽

Harlow

The day passes with a blur. I attend my classes and manage to be back in the room by one. Irelyn is here, so she must have skipped her last class.

"What are you doing here?"

"My chemistry professor canceled class today, so I finished early." She pats a seat next to her on her bed, and I know she is ready to talk. "Are you ready to fill me in?"

"Yeah. I guess so." There is just so much she doesn't know about...so much that I've hidden about myself. I know that I can trust her. I'm finally ready to share those missing pieces. I start by telling her about Phoenix. Well, everything except the D/s we partake in. Our sex life will remain private. Instead, I tell her that we're official and about last night when Desiree caught us kissing.

"I don't know what to say, Harlow. Obviously, you're

happy, so I want that for you. I just don't want you to get hurt. Phoenix's whole world is about to change. We both know how he's gotten down in the past, not to mention his hot and cold."

"I imagine we will have our ups and downs, just like any other couple. I don't expect things to be perfect." I sit on the bed next to her. "I know there will be women vying for his attention, but I'm willing to see if we can make it work."

"I guess I'm just confused. This all seems so sudden. Just a few months ago, you were withdrawn and hid behind baggy clothes and makeup. Not a single man could turn your head. You went out of your way to avoid them. Why the drastic change?"

AND THERE IT IS. MY OPENING. "IRELYN, I WAS raped."

"No. No. No. I figured it was something like that. I just didn't want it to be true. I'm so sorry. Didn't mean to push." She is a blubbering mess.

"Stop. You're fine. I want to tell you." It's not a story I like to relive, but for her, I will. She has been so supportive from the beginning with my mood swings, bitchiness, and just overall weirdness. She deserves the truth.

"It was stepdad number three. After my mom left Asher's dad, she met and married Thomas. She is completely in love with him, and her marriage to him has lasted the longest. The first six months were fine, but then he started sneaking into my room."

"Oh God, Harlow. How old were you?" Tears start to well in my eyes, but I have to continue.

"I was sixteen. It was my junior year. He threatened to beat me and to leave my mother. She was so happy with him, Irelyn. I couldn't be the cause of her to lose yet another husband. I know better now, but back then, he had me brainwashed. He knew everything to say. I became his toy. The visits at night became more and more frequent until I was a shell of my former self. I fucking endured that abuse for two years. I would tell my mother I was staying over at a friend's, just to get away from him when really I would sleep in a park or whatever place I could find." I'm full out crying now.

"Oh, Harlow." Irelyn hugs me, and she is crying with me. "You can't let him get away with this. You have to tell your mom. What if he is doing this to somebody else now?"

"I can't, Irelyn. I'm not there yet. It took a lot just to tell you, and you're my best friend. Please promise you won't say anything until I'm ready." She nods her understanding, but I know how much she hates to agree to that. "Phoenix has saved me. He makes me feel whole again. My sexuality and how much I give is on my terms. For the first time, I have a normal relationship where I'm free to share my body with someone I care about. He makes me feel sexy and desired. Even when I tried to push him away, he wouldn't give up. He saw past all the baggy clothes and makeup, just like you did. He saw me, Irelyn." She wipes the tears from her eyes.

"Okay, babe. All of this just breaks my heart, but I want you to be happy. I'm rooting for you guys. I'm glad that he is that for you—someone who can make you feel whole again. I love you, Harlow. And when you're ready to bring that sick bastard to justice, I will be there to hold your hand."

I'm so glad that I got all of that out. There are no more lies between us. The kink between Phoenix and me isn't a lie. I have to keep some stuff personal with my man.

'MY MAN.' THAT HAS A NICE RING TO IT. I WIPE MY own tears and try to put those painful memories away. I need happy thoughts. I need Phoenix.

"Do you mind if I use your car again?"

"You're going to see Phoenix again, aren't you?" She smiles and shakes her head. "You know you can," she answers, even before I can answer.

"That transparent, huh?"

"Yeah. Pretty much. What are you going to tell Asher? That you're there to visit him again?" She laughs out loud at her own joke. "You two are going to have to come clean sooner rather than later. That ruse you have going on is not going to last long."

"I know. I'll talk to him soon. It needs to come from me anyway."

"Mm-hmm. Get out of here. Go see *your man*," she teases. She hands me her keys, and I'm out the door within minutes. I'm giddy the whole drive over. This is what Phoenix does for me. He erases the pain when I'm with him. I wish I could make Asher see it that way, but there is no way in hell I'm ready to share what happened to me. He would go apeshit crazy. He needs to focus on their new record deal. I'll just tell Asher that I wanted to see him and Lily again before she leaves since I didn't stick around last night. I'll figure out how to tell him the truth, but I need time. I just hope Phoenix is happy to see me.

THE DOOR IS UNLOCKED AGAIN, SO I JUST LET MYSELF in. These guys need to really work on that. I run up the stairs. I didn't see the Escalade parked out front, but I did see Phoenix's bike. I'm hoping from the quietness that it means that they're all gone. Alone time with Phoenix would be good right now.

"Sevyn, you need to get the fuck out of here before the guys get back. You know you're supposed to wait for the green light to show up here," Phoenix growls. *Holy shit.* I pause on the steps leading to the main level on the second floor. Apparently, neither of them heard me come in, due to their heated argument. I've only heard Phoenix take this tone once before, and it was last night when he was on the phone with this Sevyn person when I came up the stairs.

"Look. I know you're pissed at me for what happened with Harlow, but I put a stop to it immediately. Don't renege on our agreement. I need you, Phoenix." I recognize that voice. Is he arguing with himself? Why is he saying he needs himself? *What. The. Fuck?* Curiosity gets the best of me, and I have to see what is going on. I'm not prepared for what I see. My whole fucking world has just been tilted on its axis. I. Can't. Breathe.

"There...There... are twooooo of you?" I stutter. What the ever-loving fuck is going on?

"Fuccccck!" I don't even know who in the hell is speaking. One of the twins pace the floor while the other takes a seat on the sofa and puts his head in his hands. I start to back away slowly. The hot and cold is starting to make sense. Apparently, I was with "Sevyn" yesterday on the sofa watching *Elementary,* and that is why Phoenix is pissed. "Harlow, wait," the one pacing says as he reaches for me.

"WHO THE FUCK ARE YOU?" I CRY. THE TEARS ARE BACK full force now. Oh, God. I kissed and dry-humped Sevyn yesterday. Have I fucked him too? Have I unknowingly slept with both brothers?

"It's me, Phoenix. And that is my brother, Sevyn," he says, pointing at his identical twin on the sofa. Shit, they're identical down to their tattoos and swagger. That can't be by accident. They have gone to great lengths to fool people, but why? I feel violated all over again. I thought I was in control of my sexuality, choosing whom I gave my body to. I don't even know whom I fucked right now. How can Phoenix be this cruel? How can he break me like this? It took courage to get to this point, and he's just undone it all in an instant. How do I come back from this? I cry even harder now.

"I figured that much, jackass. Stay the fuck away from me. You and your sick ass brother!" I shout.

"Please let me explain," he begs, reaching for me again. I dodge his grasp.

"I don't want to hear shit you have to say. You..." I can't even finish my sentence. I don't have the strength to argue with him right now. I'm about to have a total meltdown, and I'll be damned if I give him the satisfaction of seeing it. I turn and run back the way I came, as fast as my feet will carry me.

"Harlow!" I hear Phoenix call after me.

"Give her some space, Phoenix," I hear Sevyn say. It's so crazy that even their voices are identical. One thing is for certain. I hate them both for what they did to me. I find myself back in the same mental place that I'd managed to escape from two years ago. I get into the car and peel off down the street. I don't even know where I'm headed, but it is definitely in the opposite direction of the university.

EPILOGUE
Phoenix

The pain written on Harlow's face when she fled is nothing short of heartbreaking. I can't even look at Sevyn right now. He's fucked up everything. He wasn't supposed to even be here. I would have told her about my brother eventually, but we hadn't gotten to that point in our relationship. We just made it official today, for fuck's sake. Now it doesn't even matter. She gave me her trust, and she feels betrayed. I can only imagine the thoughts running through her mind. I need to find a way to fix this, but how? I haven't even told the guys I had a twin, let alone he has been here at the house as me on multiple occasions.

They're going to feel betrayed, too. This is going to destroy our chemistry for sure. I don't even know the future of Phoenix Rising at this point. Will they still want to be a band after they find out what I've been up to—Sevyn's real identity? They know him by name only. They question why he's never came around, but respected my privacy enough not to pry. This is all coming to a head, and I'm literally afraid of the outcome. I may just lose the woman who has actually come to mean something to me, and my band, in the same fucking day. I will talk to Asher first about Sevyn and try to make him understand. Our switch in and out of the house was not malicious or intended to hurt anyone, yet that is exactly what happened. This is one big cluster fuck, and I don't know if I will be able to fix it.

~

THANK YOU FOR READING PHOENIX RISING: ISSUE #1, the start of our new rock star series with a twist! We hope you loved meeting Phoenix and Harlow. Continue their journey and find out what happens next with this **SNEAK PEEK** of PHOENIX RISING: ISSUE #2

ONE-CLICK PHOENIX RISING: ISSUE **#2 now**!

SIGN UP FOR OUR WATSON & STACKS' NEWSLETTER to find out when new books release: https://www.subscribepage.com/watsonandstacksbooks

. . .

Join our *Facebook group*, **Watson & Stacks' Wicked Vixens**, for exclusive giveaways and sneak peeks at future books.

Reviews help readers find books. Please leave a review and help spread the word to those who love a unique twist on rock star romance. We greatly appreciate our readers. Thank you for your support. You rock!

SNEAK PEEK ~ PHOENIX RISING: ISSUE #2
Chapter One - Harlow

I stare into the full-length mirror in the dorm room that I used to share with Irelyn. The spring semester here at the University of Alabama starts in a few days, yet all my classes are online. I stare at the reflection of the dumbass looking back at me in the mirror, who might be about to make yet another mistake she'll regret. I can't believe I agreed to go on tour with Phoenix Rising. When I walked—no, when I stormed—away from the lake house two months ago, I swore I would never see Phoenix or his twin brother ever again. Phoenix nearly destroyed me. He let me fall for him while he and his twin brother substituted in and out of my life at their fucking convenience. Was any of it real? Hell, I don't even know who my feelings were for.

I desperately wanted to escape Alabama at that moment, but my life was here now. I had school obligations. Not to mention, I was in Irelyn's car at the time. These things kept me from running, but it was Irelyn who helped me keep my sanity. She wouldn't let me go back to being the insecure girl who hid behind dark makeup and baggy clothes. Every day was a struggle to just exist, but I took it one day at a time. Although I still hurt, the pain fades a little more with each passing day.

"Are you having second thoughts?" Irelyn asks as she comes in and catches me staring blankly in the mirror.

"Well, it's not like I'm anxious to be around Phoenix again. That part sucks, but this is not for him. I can't let him fuck up this opportunity for me." Irelyn nods approvingly.

"Smart girl," she replies. *I'm glad somebody thinks so.*

Asher invited me last month to join their tour for a month or so. He thought it would be a great experience to continue documenting their journey. This is a valuable opportunity for my aspirations as a music journalist. My peers would kill for the chance. Textbooks and the classroom can only teach so much. Because of this, I told him I would think it over. Asher never found out about my brief fling with Phoenix, if you can call it that. He would have kicked his ass, and the band's dream of a record deal would have probably been over before it started. No, Phoenix came clean about who Sevyn was and left the explanation at that. He never told the guys that he and his brother exchanged places in the house. He simply told the guys he had a twin brother, but it couldn't be made public for personal reasons. Nobody outside the band was allowed to know. The guys all respected his need for privacy, especially since it was Sevyn who connected them with Desiree. Of course, Asher wanted to keep me in the loop, so he told me after swearing me to secrecy. If he only knew how I really found out. I stayed quiet for the sake of keeping the band intact.

Surprisingly, it was Irelyn who talked me into saying yes to joining Asher on tour. She pointed out that I didn't have to stay the entire time. I only needed to stay long enough to get the gist of life behind the scenes. She pleaded with me not to let Phoenix ruin this for me.

"I LIKE THIS STRONG WOMAN STANDING HERE NEXT TO me," she continues. I snap out of my reverie. I don't know how strong I am, but we're about to see.

"We'll see," I begin. "Besides, it will give me a chance to get to know Lily. She and Asher are getting kind of serious, I think. He didn't tell me this, but he asked her to join him on the tour as well. That's huge!"

"Yeah, it is. It means no groupie pussy for him." Irelyn snickers. I don't want to even think about seeing Phoenix with all the groupies. I just have to keep telling myself that chapter of my life is closed.

"Asher's not like that anyway. He's always been a one-woman kind of guy. At least from what I've seen." I've never witnessed him having player tendencies, so that's all that matters.

"Wish more men were like him." Irelyn huffs. "Most guys just want to see how many bitches they can bang."

"What about Mike?" We met James and Mike at the club while the guys were performing one night. She and Mike have been seeing each other for about three months, a change for Irelyn. She doesn't usually keep the same guy around long. She gets bored with them quickly.

"Oh, I'm sure he's a dog like the rest of them. He just hasn't shown his true colors yet. I have my eye on him, though. Any sign of bullshit and his ass will get benched." She winks.

"You can't look for stuff, woman. Give the guy a chance." Fancy me trying to give someone relationship advice. I couldn't even sniff out if I was being played. Whatever, we can't both be pessimistic.

"Come on, girlie. We can't just stand here talking about these guys. You have a bus to get on tomorrow, and we have some shopping to do before then." She's already grabbing her purse off the bed.

"I do need to get a few things," I agree.

"Girl, you are going to be on tour with some hot-as-fuck men. I'm sure you'll get to go to some awesome celebrity parties and meet some new prospects. We can't have you looking plain Jane," she says with a giggle. "Just so you know, every break I get, I'm joining you. I'm inviting myself." We both laugh, but I know she isn't kidding.

"I like plain Jane," I tease. "It's better than being skanky. There will be enough of that, I'm sure."

"True. Okay, we'll find you a happy medium. Now come on, woman," she says, pushing me out the door.

∽

Phoenix

I TAKE IN THE SWEETNESS OF THIS BUS, AND I FEEL LIKE I need to pinch myself. Desiree spared no expense because we're hitting the road in style. It's like we have a luxury hotel on wheels.

"I take it you like?" Desiree appears behind me. I've been so busy checking out all the bus's cool features that I didn't even hear her get on. The guys are outside, loading the last of their equipment and waiting for Harlow to arrive.

"Hell yeah, I do!" I grin. "But can we afford all this? This fucker is huge." I don't even want to think about what this is hitting us for.

"The tour is sold out. You guys touring with Wild

Silence is the best move we could have made to get your name out there. Trust me, you guys can afford this, and if everything works out as planned, you all will be climbing the charts in no time."

Wild Silence is the rock band we will be opening for on the tour. They are killing the Billboard charts right now. Desiree is definitely impressing me. I have no doubt she will help get us to the top.

"I'm looking forward to it." She puts a hand on her hip, and my eyes follow. She always wears these sexy pantsuits that make it impossible for a man not to appreciate her curves. She clears her throat, and I know I've been busted.

"Your first stop is in Los Angeles, so you guys will have a long drive ahead from Alabama. You'll get there with enough time to rehearse before your first show, though. You'll also meet Ivy and the guys at that time. I'm flying there, so I'll see you guys in a few days."

"We'll be ready. I'm glad there is an area set aside for us to rehearse. I swear everything we could possibly need has been thought of."

"Yeah, I might have added some specifications for them to include." She smiles. "Just make sure you and the guys behave. Ivy is off-limits. Don't fuck this up." Before I can respond, she waves me off and heads off the bus.

Ivy performs backup vocals for Wild Silence, and she is the fucking epitome of sexy. She has short red hair and green eyes that pierce through you. She has a tattoo sleeve on her right arm and perky little tits that make every dick within a mile radius stand at attention. Not to mention, her vocals are the shit. Desiree has every right to put that warning on the table, but I don't really have any plans to smash that. That's like shitting where you sleep. My three-fuck rule has been back in full force since my incident with Harlow.

I broke her. Not intentionally, but it doesn't matter. Shit was better when I stuck to my rules. Now that I'll be on the road, one-night stands are all that I can offer. It's better this way. No attachments or expectations. It's been two months since I've seen or talked with Harlow. We never made contact after that day she walked in on Sevyn and me. I tried to call and apologize a few times before I finally gave up. She needed to move on—to heal. I was surprised when Asher proposed that she join us on the tour for a bit. He thought it would be a good experience for her music journalist major and a bonus for Lily since he had already invited her. How in the hell could I object to that when the rest of the guys were okay with it? I would look like the biggest jerk! I finally came clean, letting them know I had been hiding the fact that I had a twin, and that was enough, so I just kept my opinions to myself.

I'M GOING TO BE ME. I'M GOING TO FUCK BITCHES, AND I can't be worried about Harlow's feelings. The truth is, her leaving the way she did hurt me too. I fucking opened up to her—broke all my rules for her—and in the end, she didn't give me the benefit of the doubt. She didn't give me a chance to explain or fix it. It wasn't easy to let her in, but I did. She made me feel again and then ripped my damn heart open. No woman will ever get that chance again. The past two months have been hell, so, no woman will ever get that chance again. I didn't stop until I fucked her out of my system, and I have no intention of going back down that road, so I hope she has moved on as I have.

The Honda Accord pulling into the driveway interrupts my thoughts. She's here. She gets out of the car, and the feelings that rush through me are indescribable. I'm glad I'm alone on the bus so I can get a good look at her. Her waist-length hair is brown now—I'm guessing it's her natural color. I prefer brunettes anyway. She is wearing fitted jeans that make her ass look even more perfect. It makes me think of the last time I was balls deep in her tight pussy while my hand gripped her delectable round ass. *Fuck!* I can't let my thoughts go there. It was so easy to put her out of my mind when I didn't have to see her. She's no longer mine. I need to get a fucking grip. We need to hurry and get this bus moving. The sooner I can get my dick into some new pussy, the better.

∽

Harlow

I hug Irelyn goodbye while the guys take my suitcases aboard the bus. I don't see Phoenix yet, but I need to prepare myself. I don't know what to expect. The guys don't know we once had a thing, so how should we act around each other?

"You be strong," Irelyn whispers. "And you better call me."

"I will," I promise.

"Okay, go already before I cry," she sniffles. "I'll be at boring college parties while you're living it up with celebrities." She jokes, but I can tell she really is sad to see me go.

"Hush. You love the frat parties. Besides, you'll be joining us when you get a break. I'll call you every day."

"Sure, you will," she teases. "Okay, I'm really going now. I'm sure the guys are ready to get going."

I turn to see that everyone has boarded the bus. I hug her one more time before I let her go. I can already tell this is going to be harder than I thought.

Trepidation gnaws at me as I step onto the bus, but I plaster a smile on my face. "Sorry, guys! I didn't mean to hold you up."

"Nonsense. Get over here," Asher says, pulling me into a hug.

"Nice to see you again, princess," Killian and Ren

mock. I forgot all about that stupid nickname. It had a different ring to it coming from Phoenix, though. I look over at him, and he gives me a subtle chin lift as a way of hello. Our eyes lock for the briefest of seconds before he returns attention to his phone. His hair has grown out some, and he's even sexier than I remember.

"Where's Lily?" I ask. I need to keep my thoughts away from Phoenix.

"She is in one of the bunks taking a nap," Asher explains. "Come on, let me show you to your bunk." I follow him while taking in the opulence of everything. This bus is gorgeous—definitely quite a few classes above our dorm room.

"Wow, this is a lot of space," I gasp. There are two sets of bunks side by side, with another set directly across for a total of eight bunks. They even have little TVs in each one.

"Yeah. They are twin size. There is a master bedroom toward the back of the bus, and that is where some of our luggage is kept. The rest is stored underneath the bus. We decided it would be fair if we didn't appoint one person to get the bedroom. Instead, we'll use it to rehearse—"

"And as the designated fuck room," Phoenix adds, cutting Asher off.

He drops that bomb and walks right past us to his bunk. Apparently, his is on top of mine. *Great.*

"Shut it, Phoenix. Have some respect, man!" Asher chastises.

"Might as well open her eyes now, bro. You're the one who invited her to tag along. This isn't a daycare. We won't be filtering what we say. At least I won't."

"I didn't ask you to, jackass!" How dare he? That tag along jab stung, but I'll be damned if I let it show. It's apparent he doesn't want me here. *Noted.*

"Don't be a fucking tool, Phoenix." Asher glares at him, and the tension between the two is palpable. This is what I don't want.

"Whatever," Phoenix dismisses. He reaches up and grabs the earphones from his bunk and leaves without another word.

"I'm so sorry, Harlow," Asher starts.

"It's not a big deal. I halfway know what to expect, and it doesn't bother me. I don't want you guys to be anyone other than yourselves. I'm documenting the band's musical journey, so I sure as hell don't want a scripted one." He shakes his head, but I can tell he is starting to calm down. "It'll be okay. Promise me that you won't give me any special treatment."

"Harlow," he tries to object.

"Promise, Asher, or I'll have them turn this bus around and take me back. That's not what I'm here for."

"Fine, princess. I know you have to experience it all. It's just, to me, you're still my baby sister. I respect what you're asking, so I promise to lay off." He pulls me into a hug.

"Thank you."

"Of course. Just know the bedroom is open to anyone when we're not rehearsing. If you want to go in there for a nap, just to get away from the testosterone for a bit, or just whatever. It has a bigger walk-in shower in the master bath too. The smaller one is toward the front of the bus."

Asher grabs my hand to show me the room. Just wow. This bedroom is so luxurious. The bed looks so plush. I just want to get lost in that thread count. Oh, and the mirrors. They're everywhere. I bet some kinky shit will go down in here. My heart sinks a little when I think about that kinky shit being with Phoenix.

"It's really nice, Asher," I muster without tearing up.

"Mm-hmm. Desiree did a good job. She got this bus for us." He beams with pride. "You should check out the glass shower and Jacuzzi tub in here."

"Maybe another time. A nap really does sound good right now. Irelyn and I were up half the night talking, getting our last bit of girl time in before I left." This all feels overwhelming all of a sudden. I'm both excited and scared shitless. I can feel my unresolved feelings for Phoenix trying to resurrect themselves, and he's made it clear that he has moved on. He's already counting down the time until he can use that bedroom. I'll never sleep in there, and I don't know how to prepare myself to listen to him fucking someone else. My bunk is close to the master bedroom, so hearing what goes down in there is inevitable. I remember how much it hurt that day when I realized he fucked Irelyn's cousin, Sasha. I didn't have to listen to it, but it was enough just to know she had a piece of him. We weren't even in a relationship at the time. This is a fucking disaster waiting to happen, and I have no choice but to watch it play out. He's no longer mine.

PHOENIX RISING: ISSUE #1 PLAYLIST

Have Faith in Me - A Day to Remember
Fuck You All the Time - Jeremih
Come Undone - Duran Duran
I Wanna be Yours - Arctic Monkeys
Planes - Jeremih
Love. Sex. Riot. - Issues
Tonight (Best I Ever Had) - John Legend
Speechless - Memphis May Fire
One Way or Another - Until the Ribbon Breaks
The Dying Hymm - The Color Morale
The Worst of Them - Issues
Out of Exile - Audioslave
The Sinner - Memphis May Fire
The Downfall of Us All - A Day to Remember
Shackled Up - Alex Vargas
Scared - Mothica
Blank Space - I Prevail

OTHER BOOKS BY S.R. WATSON & RYAN STACKS

Pretty Boy Rock Series
  Phoenix Rising: Issue #1
  Phoenix Rising: Issue #2
  Phoenix Rising: Issue #3
  Reckless Ambition: Issue #1
  Reckless Ambition: Issue #2
  Reckless Ambition: Issue #3

The Playboy's Lair Duet
  Silas: A Playboy's Lair Novel – Part One
  Silas: A Playboy's Lair Novel – Part Two

Forbidden Trilogy
  Forbidden Attraction - Book #1
  Forbidden Love - Book #2
  Unforbidden - Book #3

Stand Alone

The Object of His Desire

Mister English

Peppermint Mocha Love: A Christmas Novella (written as S. Renee' ... co-authored with R.L. Harmon)

Her Favorite Christmas Gift (written as S. Renee' ... co-authored with R.L. Harmon)

Legion of Supernatural Academy Series

Quantum Entanglement: Part One

Quantum Entanglement: Part Two

Quantum Entanglement: Part Three

ABOUT S.R. WATSON

USA Today Bestselling Author, S. R. Watson, is a Texas native who currently resides in Washington with her children. She grew up reading the Sweet Valley series (Twins, High, & University) among others. Her passion for writing began in high school and continued even after earning her nursing degree and becoming an operating room registered nurse. Discovering the Twilight series and 50 Shades Trilogy, inspired her to finally share her own stories.

S. R. Watson published her first book in 2014.

When S. R. Watson is not writing, or working as an OR nurse manager, she loves to read and binge watch her favorite shows.

ABOUT RYAN STACKS

USA Today Bestselling Author, Ryan Stacks, is a Walla Walla, WA native who currently reside in Utah with his wife Anna. Most would consider him a jack of all trades. His first love is wrestling and he's wrestled his entire life. In addition to his talents on the mat, Ryan has many achievements. He's a published international cover model and he released his first book, Peppermint Mocha Love with SR Watson in December 2017. For this novella, he debuted as both an author and cover photographer. Ryan Stacks has partnered with S.R. Watson to create many more stories that'll take you for a ride.

When Ryan Stacks is not writing, he spends his time making fun TikToks, traveling, being active with the youth in his community by coaching wrestling, and helping in Young Life as a leader. In addition to his commitment to the community, Ryan has taken his fitness career to new highs as a men's physique competitor - placing top 3 at the national level.

Made in the USA
Monee, IL
19 July 2023